PEN

PATTERN FOR TERROR

HUGH PENTECOST

Carroll & Graf Publishers, Inc.
New York

First Carroll & Graf edition 1990

Carroll & Graf Publishers, Inc.
260 Fifth Avenue
New York, NY 10001

Library of Congress Cataloging-in-Publication Data

Pentecost, Hugh, 1903–
    Pattern for terror / Hugh Pentecost.—1st ed.
        p.   cm.
    ISBN 0-88184-519-1 : $14.95
    I. Title.
PS3531.H442P34   1989   89-27675
813'.52—dc20   CIP

Manufactured in the United States of America

Part One

1.

"UNCLE GEORGE! UNCLE GEORGE!"

It was a young boy's high shrill voice, raised to what sounded almost like a scream of fear. George Crowder, sitting at the table in his cabin at the south end of the New England town of Lakeview, put down his coffee cup hard and started to rise.

Then, once more—"Uncle George!"

Crowder had expected to see his ten-year-old nephew Joey Trimble that morning. It was Saturday, and Saturday morning always involved a visit from Joey, but not with this overtone of fear. Crowder walked out onto the stone terrace that fronted his cabin, and looked down the road. There was Joey, at the very entrance to the driveway, a hundred yards away, leaning against a tree and shouting for help. When Crowder appeared, Joey raised his arms in a wild beckoning and cried out again, "Uncle George!"

Crowder trotted down the path to the boy. He

couldn't see any trouble or problem as he drew closer to Joey.

"What is it, boy?"

Joey grabbed at his uncle's arm and clung to the sleeve of his jacket.

"Mr. Francis, the new English teacher at the Academy," the boy said. "He's in the ditch out there by the main road."

"Drunk?" Crowder asked.

"I don't think he's breathing," Joey said. "That means—?"

"That means he's dead if he isn't breathing," Crowder said. "Go back up to the cottage, Joey. Call Dr. Potter and tell him. Then call Sheriff Egan and tell him. Then you better call Mr. Willis at the Academy and tell him, too."

"Tell them what?"

"Just what you have told me. We need an ambulance—just in case."

The boy took off on a run and Crowder headed for the main highway. The Longview Academy is an expensive boys' boarding school which is at the heart of the town of Lakeview's existence. You didn't have to be a detective to find Mr. Francis. He was lying in the ditch beside the main road. Yesterday's thunderstorms had left the ditch full of water. Francis lay on his back in the muddy water, eyes turned skyward. He was wearing an expensive summer suit that was now soaking wet.

Crowder knelt down beside him. There was no sign of life, and Crowder couldn't detect any pulse. Alexander Francis was dead beyond any question. Crowder let the man's arm drop after searching for the nonexistent pulse, and left Francis as he was. It was clear where he had tumbled and slid down the bank into the ditch. A fatal seizure of some sort?

It is probable that George Crowder was thought of as a character by most people who got to know him in Lakeview. Born and raised there, along with his sister Esther, Crowder had gone to the local grade school. He'd then gone on to the Academy as a day student. Half a dozen local boys a year were permitted to enter the Academy as day students, thus avoiding the expenses and disciplines of being a boarder. "It's the least we can do for a town that has accepted us with such cordiality," Joshua Willis, the headmaster, often said. From the Academy Crowder went on to Yale, graduated, and then to law school. He came back to Lakeview as a young adult, opened his own law office, and launched himself on a highly successful career. Several years later he was elected county attorney, and became the prosecutor for the county. He was highly successful at this until tragedy struck. He prosecuted a man named Mullins for murder, got a conviction, and lived to see the criminal die in the gas chamber. Some months later, new evidence surfaced that showed, beyond a doubt, that Mullins had been unquestionably innocent. Crowder resigned his office as county attorney, and left town. No one knew where he went.

"Probably drinking himself to death somewhere," Hector Trimble said. Hector, married to Crowder's sister Esther, was not a fan of Crowder's.

After eight years Crowder reappeared, built a small

cabin, and settled down to do nothing of any consequence.

"Hatching his eggs," Hector Trimble suggested.

During this time Joey Trimble was growing up, a part of his uncle's life. It was a passionate admiration society.

"My Uncle George is the greatest man with a rifle or handgun in this town, in this county, or the state." "My Uncle George is the grestest crime expert almost anywhere."

"Is that how he came to send an innocent man to the gas chamber?" Hector Trimble asked his son.

"My Uncle George handled the case brilliantly," Joey said, undaunted. "It was the state police who fouled up. My Uncle George is the greatest—whatever! You name it!"

As a result of this youthful horn blowing, almost everyone in Lakeview who knew Crowder called him "Uncle George." He had never reopened his law office, never handled anyone's legal affairs. "If a man can't trust his instincts, his gut feelings," Uncle George once said, "he shouldn't fool with another man's vital problems."

But he was trusted, was asked for advice and help, and he gave it, but not in the legal framework of a court. It did not occur to Uncle George or to anyone else, except perhaps Hector Trimble, that he would be interfering in the handling of the first part of this problem of the death of young Mr. Francis, the English teacher. There was no sign of any kind of wound. No blood visible anywhere on his wet clothing.

A siren sounded down the road and it was clear

that professional help was coming, hopefully including the doctor.

Joey had evidently conveyed the information correctly because Sergeant Styles of the state police had stopped to pick up two of the people Uncle George had wanted—Dr. Potter and Sheriff Egan. Potter, a pleasant-faced, sandy-haired man with gentle blue eyes, took a quick look at the man in the ditch.

"George is right. He isn't breathing. No pulse. We better get him to Emergency."

"Any use?" Sheriff Egan asked from between his bright red mustache and beard.

"Once in a great while you can bring them back," the doctor said. "In this case, I don't think so. But the sergeant will need to know what killed him."

"What was he doing out here at seven o'clock in the morning?" Styles asked. "That's early for the Academy people."

"Going to or coming from the Academy?" Egan asked.

"Going to," Uncle George said. "See where he fell? He was headed north."

Sergeant Styles brought a stretcher from the van and he and the doctor lifted Alexander Francis's body onto it, and carried it to the van.

"Stick around, Red," Uncle George said to the sheriff. "Josh Willis should be showing up any minute. He can tell us what Francis might have been up to."

Even as he spoke a silver-gray Cadillac came up the main road from the south. Josh Willis wouldn't be driving anything but the best, Uncle George thought.

Willis was a big, heavily built man, with iron-gray hair, bushy gray eyebrows, and glasses clipped to his high-bridged nose. He got out of the car and looked around. "Police van took him?"

Uncle George nodded. "Dead, I'm afraid."

"They know why or how?" Josh Willis asked.

"Not till they've performed an autopsy. But they're interested in knowing what he was doing out here at seven in the morning."

"Regular thing with him," Willis said. "When he joined our faculty last fall, he was teaching a course in writing at the Extension department at Columbia in New York. We gave him permission to go to New York after school every Friday so he could continue with his pupils there until the end of the school year."

"He didn't have a car he could drive to New York?" Uncle George asked.

"He doesn't have a car, and he didn't want to borrow one, though we offered one. It's only half a mile from the bus station to his dormitory at the Academy. He often stayed late in New York, and he would take a bus back that got him into Lakeview about six-thirty A.M. He would walk to school—right by here."

"Party? Was he a drinker?"

"Not in the sense of alcoholism. I've never seen him take a drink anywhere in public since he has been with us. Let's go to Emergency and see what the result is."

Just as the two men were getting into the Cadillac, Joey came down the path from the cabin.

"Thanks for calling me, boy," Mr. Willis said.

"Uncle George told me who to call," the boy said. "Can I go with you? I'd like to know how it comes out."

"If your uncle approves," Willis said.

"Facts of life have to be learned," Uncle George said.

"And the facts of death?" Joshua Willis asked.

"You have to admit, Joshua, that death is a fact of life," Uncle George said.

"Mr. Francis was getting to be a friend," Joey said. "I care what happened to him."

"Oh! You didn't tell me, Joey," Uncle George said.

"It's only the last few weeks," Joey said. "I come out here every Saturday morning to see Uncle George," Joey said, explaining to Willis. "Recently I began to meet Mr. Francis coming up from town. We would just wave and say 'Hi!' and then we would stop and talk. I found out who he was and that he went into New York every Friday and came back Saturday morning. He told me about his job at the Academy, and I told him about my life—which is mostly Uncle George. He said he'd like to meet 'that fabulous uncle of yours' someday, and I said 'any Saturday morning.' I had it in mind to surprise you with him today, Uncle George. I got here first, and I saw him coming up the road, perfectly normal. He saw me and waved. And then, all of a sudden, he staggered and fell down the bank into the ditch."

"So he wasn't mugged by someone," Willis said.

"Oh, no. I saw him every step of the way," Joey said. "I ran over to where he fell, called out to him. He didn't answer or move. I kept calling to him, shaking his shoulder. Then I saw he wasn't breathing and I went for Uncle George."

"Probably a heart attack," Willis said. "Did he grab at his chest, boy?"

"I didn't see it if he did," Joey said.

Sheriff Red Egan was in the waiting room of the hospital when Uncle George, Joey, and Joshua Willis walked in.

"He's in there," Egan said, jerking a thumb toward the emergency room. "We stripped him coming over in the van. Not a bruise or scratch. Nothing. Styles and I thought he might have been mugged on his walk from the bus to the Academy. No sign of anything like that. They're going in."

"Going in?" Joey asked.

"They will do an autopsy to see what is wrong with his internal workings. Best bet is heart."

"He had no record of any heart problems," Willis said. "Our teachers all have to undergo a physical exam before they come to work for us. Francis was a hundred percent okay."

"But he is dead," Red said. "And, as Joey told me, while he was watching, Francis was walking normally and suddenly boom!"

The door to Emergency opened and Sergeant Styles came out. His face was set in a grim expression. "One for the book," he said.

"Heart?" Red Egan asked.

"In the sense that it stopped working, yes. But why it stopped working is the story."

"Why?"

"You read in the paper recently about some guy

who dropped dead and they found a condom filled with drugs in his stomach?"

"Drugs?" Red Egan asked.

"He wasn't carrying drugs for his own use," Styles said. "What he had on him was worth quite a few thousand bucks at street prices. He was a courier for illegal drug merchants."

"Not Alex Francis!" Joshua Willis said.

"He wasn't using a condom to carry the stuff," Styles said. "He used a little plastic bag you might get in a pharmacy for carrying medicine. It split open and Francis collected a massive overdose of heroin or cocaine. The lab hasn't said which, yet."

"If it's as big as a condom, how do they get it in and out?" Red Egan asked.

"Big as a giant condom," Styles said. "Doc Potter says it wouldn't be easy for him to swallow."

"Ugly!" Red Egan said.

"Ugly and deadly," Styles said.

Joshua Willis was shaking his head from side to side, "Alex Francis wasn't working for drug dealers, I'd swear to that."

"Don't swear till we find out," Styles said. "You have a lot of rich kids at the Academy, and they have rich families. Your Mr. Francis went to New York every Friday, and could come back each time with drug supplies for customers. There is no way you could know, Mr. Willis. Federal agents stopping him wouldn't find anything in his clothes, his briefcase, or in whatever else he might be carrying. There is nothing that would show he had a gutful of drugs."

"How would he get it out when he got here?" Egan asked.

"An emetic," Styles said. "Out the way it went in."

"Maybe I can be of some help," Uncle George said. "I've never told anyone what I did when I left town after the Mullins case. I had to do something positive or go crazy. I joined up with the federal government's drug team. I made a lot of strange contacts. I might be able to trace Mr. Francis's contacts in New York. While I'm at that, you might be trying to trace who he was delivering to here."

"I don't understand why he would get involved," Joshua Willis said. "He was well paid here at the Academy."

"How well paid?" Uncle George asked.

"About five hundred dollars a week, plus board and room," Willis said. "He was a first-class teacher."

"The stuff he was carrying could easily have been worth a year's salary for him each trip," Uncle George said.

"The bank will tell us if he was depositing more than his salary," Willis said.

"I'd say it was unlikely he was depositing extra money here. A loose tongue, some questions, and he would have been in big trouble. I'd guess his drug fees were put in a separate account in New York. Not under the name of Alexander Francis—but Smith, Jones, or Brown. Hard to trace. I'll give it a try," Uncle George said.

"Uncle George is the best detective there is anywhere," Joey said.

"My nephew is subject to overstatements," Uncle George said.

"But we'll be damn glad of your help," Styles said.

"I'll give it a shot," Uncle George said, "but under certain conditions."

"Conditions?" Sergeant Styles asked.

"Don't report this to the press the way it is. I suggest you report that Francis died of a heart attack. Mention drugs, and the people we're after will be forewarned, prepared, and go into deep hiding."

"The hospital records can't be falsified," Styles said.

"But they don't have to be shown to anyone who asks," Uncle George said.

"I guess that can be managed," Styles said. "And it makes sense."

"And Mr. Willis, this goes for the Academy, too. Or any friends of Francis."

"I don't see why not," Joshua Willis said.

"Good. Now, the name of this department where Francis was teaching at Columbia in New York?"

"The Extension department," Willis said. "It's not for students in the college or university. Anybody in the city, you or I, who wants a course in almost anything can find it in Extension. Alex Francis's record there was so good—teaching literature and writing—that we approached him. He agreed, and decided he could complete the term in Extension that he was teaching. It was every Friday night and it didn't interfere with his schedule with us. We don't have any night classes at the Academy."

"Do you know the name of his boss at Columbia?"

"David Ash. He is the head of the English department in Extension."

"Same story everywhere," Uncle George said, "a heart attack."

"I'd better get back in there and tell them how we're playing it," Styles said. "Heart attack, no drugs. Doc Potter isn't going to like it. He gets along awfully well with *The Lakeview Press*. He isn't going to like lying to them."

"He'll like nailing a brutal killer, won't he?" Joshua Willis asked.

"He can talk truthfully to anyone who matters," Uncle George said, "local police, state police, federal drug cops. Just don't spread the truth to the general public. That would alert the people we're after."

"No chitchat to your friends, Joey," Red Egan said.

Uncle George rested his hand on the boy's shoulder. "You can count on Joey being the soul of discretion," he said. "Now we had better discuss who will handle what part of the next action."

2.

THE ONLY PERSON WHO DIDN'T HAVE A REGULAR LO-
cal routine to follow was Uncle George. It was decided he should be the one to cover New York. He
wouldn't be missed in Lakeview, and he had connec-
tions that might be helpful with the drug end of
things there. He made a couple of phone calls to his
contacts and headed in his white Jeep for the Big
Town.

An old friend in New York was Captain Mark Lewis
of the federal drug force.

"If I start asking about Alex Francis at Columbia
Extension, it will be a dead giveaway," Lewis said.
He and Uncle George were eating lunch in a little
chophouse in the Times Square area. "As a Lakeview
citizen, it won't seem suspicious if you ask about
him. He's part of your town. They'll want to write
something nice about him in your local press."

"Who should I talk to first?" Uncle George asked.

"David Ash, head of the English Department where Francis had a legitimate job," Lewis said. He brought his hand down hard on the table. "Ever since that condom story broke a few weeks back, there must be hundreds of jerks carrying drugs around in their guts. I wish to God that that had been kept secret!"

Uncle George hadn't been able to make an appointment with Ash by phone.

"I'm in and out of my office all day," Ash told him. "You will just have to come in and wait for me. It won't be too long. Care to tell me what it is about?"

"I'd prefer to wait till I see you," Uncle George said. "It is something that will be important to you, I'm afraid."

Uncle George parked his Jeep in a garage on upper Broadway, and went to Ash's office, which overlooked South Field, the long-ago sports center for Columbia College. When Ash arrived, Uncle George was struck by an almost comical relationship between the man's name and his appearance. David Ash had ash-blond hair. He was a somewhat tough-looking man in his forties, Uncle George guessed, with very bright blue eyes.

"I couldn't have kept you waiting too long, Mr. Crowder," Ash said, glancing at his watch. "What can I do for you?"

"I'm afraid I have some rather painful information for you," Uncle George said. "It has to do with one of your faculty members, Alexander Francis."

"Oh, brother, what has Alex been up to?"

"I'm sorry to tell you, he is dead."

"Dead!"

"Heart attack, about seven o'clock this morning."

"Oh, my God!" Ash appeared to be genuinely upset, not in any way frightened as he might be if he suspected the real truth.

"I live in Lakeview, the New England town where Lakeview Academy is located. Francis had struck up a friendship with a ten-year-old nephew of mine, and they were in the habit of meeting just outside my house on Saturday mornings when Francis came back from teaching his course here. Francis walked from the bus terminal in town to the Academy, and he and Joey would meet just outside my place and exchange the time of day. This morning Joey saw him coming up the road, all perfectly normal. Then, suddenly, Francis staggered and fell into a ditch beside the road. Joey called me. Francis wasn't breathing when I got to him. No pulse. The local doctor pronounced him dead of heart failure."

"It's hard to believe. He looked to be in such very good shape."

"I came here to find out what I could about him," Uncle George said. "The Academy records, except for his educational history, are pretty sketchy. Family, friends?"

"I don't know that our records will be any better than yours. We are mostly interested in educational histories, too. I know Alex wasn't married and that his parents were both killed some years ago in a plane crash. I don't know about aunts and uncles."

The adult student body was a perfect field for drug dealers, Uncle George thought.

"Personal friends here?" he asked.

"There is one personal friend," Ash said. "A lady. This is going to be a killer for her. She and Alex were

17

very close. She'll want to talk to you." He reached for the phone on his desk. "Sally? Send someone over to South Hall, Leona Boyd is teaching a class in room 17F. Tell her it's an emergency. Have her send her pupils home and then report to me."

"You're suggesting Francis and this Boyd woman are—were—lovers?" Uncle George asked.

"That certainly is the impression most of us have," Ash said. "Francis's class was at seven o'clock on Friday nights. Understand, he started this course a year ago. When he signed up at Lakeview he would normally have quit here. But his pupils let out such a yowl that we arranged with the Academy to let him come back here on Friday evenings. That would all have been over next month. It seemed to work out very well. His class was over at eight o'clock. He could have taken a bus back to Lakeview that would have gotten him there about eleven at night. He didn't. He met with Leona and they were usually together until the early bus left in the morning. She has an apartment not far from our campus." Ash shrugged. "They didn't spend the winter evenings on a park bench!"

Leona Boyd and Alex Francis must have been a handsome couple. The lady, when she arrived, was an eyeful. Long dark hair, an inviting smile, a figure that would have been sensational on a stage. A man who had this woman would have been envied, Uncle George thought.

"Hi, Dave," she said, as she walked in. "What is the emergency?"

"This is Mr. George Crowder, Miss Leona Boyd," Ash said.

"Call me Leona," the girl said, holding out her hand. "Everyone does."

"Everyone calls me Uncle George, for reasons that are too complicated to go into." Uncle George said. "I have some rather shocking information for you, Leona. Why don't you sit down?"

Leona, her face suddenly serious, dropped into a chair beside Ash's desk.

"It's about Alex," Ash said. He looked at Uncle George.

"I understand he was close to you," Uncle George said.

"Was?" The lively voice was suddenly strained.

"Alex Francis died of a heart attack early this morning."

"Oh, no!" Leona said. She covered her face with her hands, to hide instant tears.

Uncle George told the story he had told Ash—Joey seeing Francis apparently struck down by heart failure.

"It doesn't seem possible," Leona said, her shoulders shaking. "I saw him off on the bus to Lakeview this morning. He was fine, then."

"That's the way heart attacks go," Uncle George said. "Suddenly, unexpected."

"I just can't believe it!"

"I'm sorry, Leona."

"Sorry! Oh, my God!"

Ash got up from his desk chair. "I have to notify the big brass down the hall," he said. "I know Mr. Crowder has some questions he wants to ask you, Leona. I'll leave you two."

"I'm sorry to load you with questions, Leona," Uncle George said, when he and the young woman were alone. "But Ash suggested you might be able to tell me things I need to know."

"Need to know? What kind of things, Uncle George?"

"We have no record of anyone to notify," Uncle George said. "According to Ash, Alex's parents are dead."

"Yes. A plane crash—about ten years ago, I think."

"Brothers and sisters?"

"Not that he ever mentioned."

"How long had you known him, Leona?"

"He came here to teach about a year and a half ago. I was already on the teaching staff. I teach stage and film acting. Alex came to see one of the plays my class put on for the students. It was *Cat on a Hot Tin Roof.* He approached me after the performance and said how great he thought it had been. What happened then was pure electricity. He invited me to have a drink with him. It was like that." She snapped her fingers. "We didn't have to discuss it. I took him back to my apartment and we were—together forever, I thought."

"Marriage in the offing?"

"Everything was so marvelous we didn't want to change it in any way. Too risky. I suppose that sometime later we might have thought of it."

"You were, in effect, living together?"

"Until Alex took the job at your Academy. Then I only saw him one day a week."

"Strange move for anyone so much in love to make," Uncle George said.

"We *were* thinking of the future," Leona said. "Recommendations from the Academy and from Dave Ash could almost certainly get Alex a job here at the university. That is where his work future lay. So we agreed to endure the separation for a year. If he chose to stay at the Academy, I would have moved up into that area to be close. We *might* have married. Of course there were holidays—Christmas, Easter, and school vacations, too."

"But your recent routine was—?"

"Alex came down from Lakeview on Friday afternoon. I met him at the bus terminal and took him to my apartment for an early supper—and—and lovemaking. Then he went to his class. It ended at eight o'clock, and he might stay for another fifteen minutes to talk to some of his students, answer questions. I'd wait for him."

"At your apartment?"

"No. At the classroom building. We'd leave there together, go back to my place, and live like people in love until it was time for him to take the early morning bus home. I'd go to the terminal with him, and then it was goodbye until the next Friday."

"It was like that yesterday?"

"Like always," the girl said.

If she is telling the truth, Uncle George thought, there was no time when Alex Francis could have taken on his cargo of drugs. Of course, if she was part of the operation, she could have been very personally involved in the drug deal.

Her grief and pain seemed to be so real, it was hard to believe she was faking. There was one thing she may not have known. She couldn't know about his trip back to Lakeview on Saturday morning. There was a place he could have stopped, taken his load of drugs aboard, and taken the next bus on to Lakeview.

That was the only way it could be if she wasn't involved in the whole scam. Where he would deliver his cargo was not visible from this end. It could have been almost anywhere in Lakeview. That was the next geographic area that had to be covered.

"What will be done about a funeral?" Leona asked.

"Unless he left a will with instructions in it, I suspect friends like you, Leona, will have to come up with that decision. He ever talk about it?"

"My God, Mr. Crowder, we never talked about dying. The only thing we ever thought of was living—living together. Who should I get in touch with in Lakeview who will know what I should do? Where is Alex now?" the girl asked.

"He's in the emergency room of the Lakeview hospital. The doctor in charge is Dr. Potter. Of course, there's always me, Leona. I can give you my phone number, you give me yours and we can stay in touch."

"You're going back there tonight?" Leona asked.

"Right now," Uncle George said. "I have a car, that white Jeep down the block."

"Could I go with you?" Leona asked. "I'd like to be where Alex is to see that everything that should be done for him is done."

"Your company would be a pleasure."

Twenty minutes later they were on the road, slow at first because the roads out of the city were crowded with late-day travelers. Their conversation was casual. He told her again how Joey had seen Francis collapse, that an autopsy was performed to make sure of the cause of death.

"No question it was a heart attack?" Leona asked.

22

PATTERN FOR TERROR

"Not that I know of," Uncle George said, looking straight ahead into the stream of traffic.

"It's hard to believe. He was so actively alive, never any mention of any trouble at any time."

It was just after seven in the evening when they reached the familiar territory of Lakeview, and Uncle George headed the Jeep toward the road to his cottage. As he turned into his own driveway, he was surprised to see a light burning in his living room window. Joey, he thought. Joey had a key to the cottage.

"A visitor," Uncle George said. "Probably my nephew."

He stopped the Jeep right by the door and got out. The front door wasn't locked and he walked in, Leona following him.

"Joey!" he called out.

There was no answer, no sound of anyone else. Uncle George saw that the desk lamp on his table had been moved out of place and was resting on a sheet of white writing paper. He walked over and picked up the paper. There was a note written to him.

Crowder:

> Back off and persuade your friends to back
> off if you have any hope of seeing your
> nephew, Joey, alive again.

No signature. Uncle George reached for the phone and dialed a familiar number. His sister Esther answered.

"It's George, Es. Is Joey there?"

"No, he isn't. I supposed he was with you."

"I've been in New York. Just got back. There was a light on in my cottage. I thought Joey was here or had been here."

"He hasn't been here all afternoon," Esther said. "Hector is furious that he didn't let us know he wouldn't be home for supper."

"I'll be right over," Uncle George said.

"You'll be setting yourself up for a 'Hector session,' " Esther said.

"Maybe I've earned it!"

He turned and saw Leona looking at the note he had dropped on his desk.

"I'm sorry," she said. "I see how shaken you are. What does it mean?"

"It's a pattern for terror," Uncle George said, his voice unsteady. "Let me tell you something, lady. If you know what this is all about, and you are in any way involved in harming Joey, I will shoot you right between your baby-blue eyes."

3.

"MR. CROWDER!" LEONA SHOUTED.

"You probably don't need an explanation," Uncle George said. "And you are laughing at me privately!"

"I don't understand a word you're saying!" Leona said.

"If you are pretending," Uncle George said, "just remember it won't matter to me that you're a woman. I will polish you off without a moment's hesitation if Joey is hurt."

"Please tell me what you are talking about!" Leona cried out.

"Francis didn't die of a heart attack," Uncle George said.

"What, then?" Leona's voice was shaken.

"An overdose of heroin. He was carrying heroin from some drug dealer internally. In his stomch. The plastic bag in which the drug was carried must have

25

ruptured and Francis died as a result, almost instantly."

"Alex was carrying drugs? That doesn't make any sense," Leona said.

"You obviously know whether it does or doesn't," Uncle George said. "He was your lover. The unshakable fact is there was a massive overdose of heroin in his gut! This note *was* written. I suspect if it is revealed that you are part of it, you will get a life sentence in prison. Hurting Joey will not seem like too great a risk for you, and probably too dangerous for the others. What is too great a risk for me is to do what they instruct me to do in that note—back off. That way Joey has no one going for him. We're going to town to talk to the police. You may convince them, even me, that you are not involved. Then you can help us."

"How?"

"By telling us all there is to know about Alex Francis. Let's get moving."

The pain of it was almost more than Uncle George could take. Joey was the dearest person on earth to him—a helpless ten-year-old threatened with God knows what kind of terror at the hands of a gang of monsters. Uncle George's hand on Leona's arm wasn't gentle as he almost dragged her out to the Jeep.

"I swear I don't know what this is all about," the girl said, as he pushed her into the passenger seat.

"I hope that is true—for your sake and mine," he said. "I wouldn't like to have to force you to talk!"

The Jeep raced along the road toward town at a greater speed than it should have been driven. Uncle George's knuckles showed white as he gripped the steering wheel. The woman sat huddled beside him, her face buried in her hands. As the Jeep headed into the main street of Lakeview, Uncle George's foot jammed down on the brakes and the Jeep slowed to a crawl. At the next corner was the red brick building that housed the Lakeview Pharmacy. Hector, Esther, and Joey Trimble lived in an apartment on the second floor. The store, which Hector owned and managed, would be closed now, but Esther and Hector would be upstairs, waiting for Joey to show up. God help them, they may have seen him for the last time.

"Joey's parents live here," Uncle George told Leona. "I've got to tell them what has happened. You're coming with me for whatever you can offer."

"Oh, my God, Mr. Crowder, I keep telling you—"

"I know you do. So does that note. It keeps telling me what will happen to Joey if we don't turn our backs on a crime and the criminals responsible for Joey's survival. Perhaps you can make Hector and Esther feel safer than I can."

The Jeep stopped in front of the unlighted pharmacy. It was after eight o'clock, after closing time on a normal Saturday.

Uncle George got out of the Jeep, still holding Leona's wrist. As they crossed the sidewalk toward the side door, it opened and Esther and Hector Trimble stepped out.

"Saw you coming," Uncle George's sister said. "Any sign of Joey?"

"I don't know where he is," Uncle George said. "But I think I know what kind of trouble he may be in."

"Because you got him there?" Hector asked.

"I suppose you could say that and be right for once," Uncle George said. "This is Miss Leona Boyd. She's not here of her own free will."

"Who would be with you of their own free will?" Hector asked.

"Oh, Hector, stop it!" Esther said. "What is the story, George? Joey is more than two hours late getting home."

"Has Joey mentioned a new friend to you, Es? A teacher at the Academy named Alexander Francis?"

Esther nodded. "A teacher at the Academy who comes up from New York every Saturday morning on the early bus? He's been meeting Joey somewhere out your way, George. Just a hello and pass the time of day. Joey seems very pleased with the situation."

"Miss Boyd is Alex Francis's girlfriend," Uncle George said. "This morning Joey was waiting for Francis outside my cabin, saw him coming, when suddenly Francis waved to him, staggered, and fell into the ditch beside the road. Joey called to me for help. Francis was dead. Not breathing, no pulse. Joey went into my place and phoned Dr. Potter, Red Egan, and the state police. They all came promptly. Francis was dead. We all assumed he suffered a heart attack. There were no signs he had been mugged or attacked in any way walking from the bus depot."

"Joey must have been badly shocked," Esther said. "He liked Mr. Francis a lot."

"We were all shocked after Dr. Potter performed an autopsy on the body. The man had been carrying drugs—heroin—in his stomach. The plastic pouch it was in, which Francis must have swallowed to carry, had ruptured and he died as a result."

"A way to smuggle it?" Hector asked. "I read of something like that—a man using a condom, or a balloon."

"They have to believe that he was a paid smuggler," Uncle George said.

"So what has that got to do with Joey?" Hector asked.

"I located Miss Boyd through the Extension department at Columbia," Uncle George said. "It seemed likely she would know how Francis handled his dealings."

"And Joey?" Hector asked, his voice grim.

"He stayed at the hospital here when I went to New York. He hoped there might be something useful he could do for his dead friend."

"So you haven't seen him since you got back?"

"I haven't seen him but I've heard of him," Uncle George said. He took the folded note out of his pocket. "This was in my cabin, waiting for me. I don't want you or Es to touch it, Hector. It already has Miss Boyd's and my fingerprints screwing it up."

Hector and Esther Trimble read the threatening message as Uncle George held it in front of them. Esther's voice broke in a little sob. Hector spoke, his voice harsh.

"And so you will back off," he said.

"I'm not sure," Uncle George said.

"With Joey's life at stake?"

"Oh, George!" Esther cried.

"Joey's life is at stake whichever way we play it," Uncle George said. "If we stop looking for the men who have him, they still can't let him go. He knows who they are. Whether or not we back off has nothing to do with Joey's safety. They'll try to use him a second time if we don't back off, by somehow letting one of us speak to him, on the phone, of course. They will make the same threat. But they will have given us a little time. We may just get on their trail before it is too late. I promise you I won't back off if Joey has been hurt. I've told Miss Boyd, I'll be out to kill."

"I don't have the greatest confidence in your detective abilities," Hector said. "Remember the time you sent the wrong man to the gas chamber. It was the news of the town!"

"But you don't know if I used my detective skills during the years I was away from here," Uncle George said.

"If you did, it didn't make headlines."

Inquiry on the phone in the pharmacy determined that Dr. Potter was still at the hospital. The others, Red Egan, Sergeant Styles of the state police, and Captain Lewis of the federal drug force, had all moved on to the state police headquarters just a block or two away. They had left a message for Uncle George to look for them there. He headed for the meeting in the Jeep, with Leona Boyd apparently no longer reluctant. She didn't have to be dragged into Sergeant Styles's office. The law was waiting for them. Uncle George described his meeting with David Ash at Columbia Extension and the introduction of Leona Boyd into the picture. He also told them about the threatening note, which was promptly delivered to an officer trained in fingerprint work.

"I told my sister that we can't back off," Uncle

George said, and he gave his friends the same arguments he had given to Esther.

"You're right, of course," Captain Lewis said. "They can't release the boy while they're walking around free."

"I don't understand why," Leona said. "If Mr. Crowder's nephew was delivered to him in the next five minutes, why wouldn't he back off?"

"That's a hopeful dream, Miss Boyd," Lewis said. "They won't turn him loose because, as Mr. Crowder just explained, he can identify them."

"He can describe some faces, but between here and New York there must be millions of faces that would fit those descriptions," Leona said.

"I think the odds are good that Joey can put names with those faces," Captain Lewis said. "I am here because my department has reason to believe that drugs were being delivered to the town of Lakeview. I arrived as soon as I could after hearing Mr. Francis, a courier, had dropped dead in a roadside ditch. Let me tell you, the two main markets for drug users are among young people and very rich older people. Lakeview has both of them—at the Academy and among a majority of the adult residents. We could help Joey identify them."

"What Francis was carrying was not enough for a group of people," Sergeant Styles interrupted. "He was, we think, carrying for one very rich addict. Someone who could pay him a fancy fee. So we have such a person in Lakeview. A rich kid at the school, or a rich resident who has some influence at the Academy. That man knows who Mr. Crowder is— Uncle George, Joey's hero, and a man who could have some influence with my people, with the police. They seize Joey and it's instantly apparent that Joey knows who they—or the man—is. Joey knows everyone in this town and where they live. All he'd have to do is report where he was held. If he can't name his jailer, he can say where he was held. End of the ballgame."

"And my Alex was involved in a criminal enterprise?" Leona asked.

"Beyond a doubt in my mind," Lewis said. "And the kidnapper can't afford to have Joey report where he's been."

"Which would reveal the kidnapper," Red Egan said. "We can't back off or the boy is done for. His only chance is that we can find him before it's too late."

"And to do this, Miss Boyd," Sergeant Styles said, "we need you to answer some questions about Alexander Francis."

Uncle George didn't think he could detect even a touch of anxiety in Leona Boyd as she waited for what was coming. Captain Lewis wasn't a bullying or overbearing type.

"You were very close to Alexander Francis, Miss Boyd?"

"I am—was—was—his woman."

"But you only spent time with him once a week?"

"That has been true since he came to work at the Academy. Before that, we shared an apartment in New York. We were like man and wife."

"And when he came up here to work at the Academy?"

"It became more complicated," Leona said. "We

weren't married. You don't live together at a fancy boys' school. Alex made a deal with Mr. Willis, the headmaster. If things worked out during the next term while Alex was going to be commuting to New York once a week—if the Academy wanted him to stay on permanently—then Alex and I would be married during the summer vacation and move into residence quarters for married faculty at the school. But as far as Alex and I are—were—concerned, we are—were—married, in spirit, in emotion."

"I understand. I'm sorry how it has worked out," Captain Lewis said. "But with that kind of relationship you wouldn't say if Francis was involved with drugs, would you?"

"I would say he wasn't," Leona said. "Flatly and all the way. It isn't possible Alex could have been involved with taking or transporting drugs without my knowing it."

"There is no question that they found drugs in his stomach," Lewis said.

"Does it occur to you, Captain, that Alex may have ingested those drugs by accident?"

"No, it doesn't, Miss Boyd. How would you swallow something the size of a giant hot dog by accident? Your Mr. Francis knew exactly what he was carrying in his gut."

It was a pretty unshakable argument, Uncle George thought.

"We are missing something somewhere," Leona said. "I knew Alex far too well to believe for one instant that he was taking or selling drugs."

"What about Francis's life at the Academy?" Red Egan asked. "He must have talked to you about it,

Miss Boyd. Had he made friends here, close friends of any sort?"

"I don't think Alex was close to anyone but me," the girl said. "But there was a Latin teacher and his wife that he spoke about with some enthusiasm. Alex and Stanley Clark had belonged to the same fraternity in college. Not the same college—Alex was Columbia, Clark was Penn. Not the same fraternity chapter, but it was a bond between them. Mrs. Clark is part of the staff in the Academy library, and they have a residence cottage on campus here. The Clarks invited Alex for a meal once or twice a week. Digger—that's Clark's nickname—drove Alex to the bus station quite often on Friday after school. It was late in the day for Alex to try to walk it."

"He didn't have a car?" Red Egan asked.

"He has a car, but I have it," Leona said.

"But you never picked him up or drove him back to the Academy on Saturday mornings?"

"We enjoyed what we had together after his Friday night class at Extension. I could not have left my own job in time to drive up here to Lakeview to get him on Friday afternoons. He preferred to spend all the time we had together in New York on Friday nights and early Saturday mornings."

"Francis didn't mention meeting Clark when he got back here on Saturday mornings?" Captain Lewis asked.

"The only person he ever mentioned on a regular basis was Mr. Crowder's young nephew Joey Trimble. 'A wonderful kid—great imagination—like an old friend, and only ten years old.' "

It was almost like a psychic coincidence. The phone

rang on Sergeant Styles's desk. He answered by just speaking his name. He looked up quickly. "For you, Mr. Crowder." As Uncle George reached for the phone, Styles made a circular gesture with his forefinger. Uncle George read it correctly. Styles was going to amplify the call so that they could all hear it.

"George Crowder here," Uncle George said.

"Well, Crowder, I know you got our message. Are you and your flat-footed friends deciding what to do about it?"

"Who is this?" Uncle George asked.

"Wouldn't you like to know?" An almost boyish giggle went with the question. "I'm going to let you hear Joey's voice so you'll know he's all right for now. But only for now, Crowder. Back off! All of you!"

Uncle George's face was rock hard, but his voice sounded unsteady. "Joey boy?"

"Uncle George!" It was Joey's high-pitched voice, obviously frightened. "Friday on Saturday," he said.

The jailer's voice broke in. "He wasn't to try to give you a message, Crowder. Tell him to do exactly what we tell him or he's going to regret it. He evidently thinks he knows something about Friday and Saturday. It would be a mistake for him to try to pass it on to you. Wise him up!"

"Joey!" Uncle George called out. He heard a whimpering sound but Joey didn't speak. "Joey, do what they tell you. This isn't a time to be extra brave." The dial tone sounded. The person on Joey's end had hung up.

"Oh, wow!" Red Egan said.

" 'Friday and Saturday,' " Captain Lewis said. "He could probably give us the whole ballgame."

"Probably," Uncle George said. "But that isn't what he said. He said 'Friday on Saturday.' "

"Doesn't make sense," Sergeant Styles said.

"Not to you, Sergeant, but I think Joey was sending me a message. Red, you know that I amuse myself by playing the guitar. Joey and I have a routine: old popular songs that were written and sung long before Joey was born. There is one he particularly likes.

> "Where did Robinson Crusoe go
>   With Friday on Saturday night?

"Notice Friday *on* Saturday?"
"Where did they go?" Red Egan asked.
Uncle George sang the tune, softly.

> "Every Saturday night
>   They would start in to roam
>   And on Sunday morning
>   They'd come staggering home.
>   Now on that island with cannibal trimmin',
>   Where there are wild men,
>   There must be wild women.
>   So that's where Robinson Crusoe went
>   With Friday on Saturday night."

"My father used to play that on the piano," Mark Lewis said. "You and he should get together and form a vaudeville act."

"But why would Joey, in his trouble, think of that old song?" Sergeant Styles asked.

"At age eight Joey wondered where Crusoe and Friday would have gone on Saturday night if they had lived here in Lakeview," Uncle George said. "The only reason I could think was to remind me of the place he chose—the Cogswell sisters' house."

"Dolly and Molly Cogswell?" Red Egan asked.

"A couple of wild women, as Joey saw them. Always with a house full of wild men in 'cannibal trimmin'.'"

"Mostly men, too. Could be cannibals, I suppose. But what was Joey trying to tell you?"

"Perhaps that that's where he is. At the Cogswells'."

"Why would he be there?" Captain Lewis asked.

"Because they are part of your drug group?" Uncle George said.

"Was Joey friends with these Cogswell sisters?" Lewis asked.

"Joey gets to be friends with anyone he knows," Red Egan replied.

"The Dolly Sisters, we call 'em. They're not far, perhaps three or four hundred yards from my place," Uncle George said. "Between my place and the Academy is the road to the Dolly Sisters', which is down on the lake. Big stone house with flags flying and pennants on the dock.

"Joey must have seen the Cogswells going and coming almost every day of his life, waved to them, but Dolly and Molly aren't the kind of girls who would waste time on a country kid."

"If you're right about his message, George, the girls may live to regret that," Red Egan said.

"And so the next move?" Captain Lewis asked.

"Can we take it just a little easy, Captain?" Uncle George asked. "The person who talked to us knew that I'd been to my place and picked up the threatening note. Doesn't that suggest I was being watched? They knew you were all here. We blink an eyelid toward the Cogswell place, and Joey, if that's where he is, will be in the severest kind of trouble."

"What has all this got to do with my Alex?" Leona Boyd asked.

"It fits like a key in a lock, girl," Uncle George said. "Your Mr. Francis walked home from the bus station every Saturday morning. No car to pick him up. Take him down on Friday yes, but not pick him up on Saturday. Walking, he cruises into Joey and they become friends. He walks on a few hundred yards, and there he can turn into the Cogswells' road and deliver his cargo to them."

"Fits like a glove," Captain Lewis said.

"Joey wouldn't know that. He'd have mentioned it to me if he did. He would have said something like, 'Mr. Francis has gone to follow Crusoe and Friday.' It would have been too good a joke for him to miss," Uncle George said.

"So we just sit here and do nothing?" Sergeant Styles asked, his voice angry. This was his town.

"It will be dark in forty-five minutes," Uncle George said. "We don't even turn our noses toward the Cogswells' till after dark. They won't be able to see us coming then, and I don't think they expect us. I think Joey slid his clue past them."

"Bless the boy," Red Egan said.

38

PATTERN FOR TERROR

"And save him," Uncle George said, his voice not steady yet.

"We have to find out exactly where they are holding him before we make a serious move," Red Egan said. "They can knock him off the minute a floorboard creaks."

Uncle George nodded somberly. "The drug traffic is going to go on for years no matter what happens here today. No matter what happens to Joey. Somehow whether the Cogswell sisters do or don't get their heroin delivered on time doesn't matter very much to me. Joey is what matters. Joey in the hands of bloodthirsty crackpots!"

Who was to be in charge of the operation, whatever it was to be, had to be decided. Sergeant Styles, of the state police, seemed the logical one; or Captain Lewis from the federal drug force in New York and a specialist in the drug rackets; or Red Egan, the local sheriff who knew everybody in town and the geography of the area like the back of his hand. But somehow all of these men decided that Uncle George, with something so personal at stake, deserved special consideration.

Captain Lewis said it about as clearly as it could be put: "I think we should agree that Crowder have veto power over whatever we decide to do. He has so much to lose, personally. How do you think this is all being handled, George?"

Uncle George looked up as though he were surprised to be asked. "If Miss Boyd is telling the truth, and I'm beginning to think she is," Uncle George said, "the routine was simple. Francis didn't contact anyone in New York. He took that early morning bus for Lakeview. No friends on the way to the bus, as Miss Boyd has told us. But at the bus stop, he meets someone he was expecting. The drugs are passed to him and he swallows them, perhaps at a rest stop. The other man gets off the bus before it reaches Lakeview. The bus driver should remember anything so regular and could identify that second man for us. Meanwhile we are being watched. Long before we had given them any cause, they knew when I came back to Lakeview after my eight-year abdication that I'd been connected with drug traffic prevention work in New York. Was I coming home on my own, or was I under orders to keep an eye out for them? So I was watched, my routine checked. My affection for Joey recognized and noted. If they wanted to slow me down, Joey would be the key piece."

"But you had nothing like that on your mind?" Captain Lewis asked.

"Nothing at all," Uncle George said. "I'd quit the government cold! Francis wouldn't know that, but he knew he should be careful of me. He walked from the bus terminal, met Joey in front of my house, had their time of day, and Francis walked on and turned into the Cogswells' without Joey knowing a thing about it. He pukes up thousands of dollars worth of drugs, and moves on after, perhaps, collecting his pay then and there! It could be that way, couldn't it, Miss Boyd?"

Leona had been listening, the whole time shaking her head in a negative fashion. But now that Uncle George had finished, she sat very still, looking straight at him.

PATTERN FOR TERROR

"Knowing my man, it's difficult for me to say yes to your question, Mr. Crowder. But, yes, it could have been managed the way you suggest without my knowing. Why he should keep it from me, even though it was a criminal act, I don't know. We trusted each other right down to the end of the line."

"He was building a substantial future for you," Uncle George said. "You wouldn't have to lie if you didn't know, when some creep asked you the wrong questions."

"He never mentioned meeting someone on the bus those Saturday mornings?" Red Egan asked.

"Never!"

Uncle George glanced out the office window, the town still alight with the last of the sun.

"Count on it that we're being watched until it becomes too dark to see us," Captain Lewis said. "We will have to wait to make it more difficult for them. Then we plant some men at the roadway entrance to the Cogswell sisters' place, and while they watch us there, we try to slide someone in from the lakeside."

"I don't think we should count on a bush-league mistake from them," Uncle George said.

"I've fished all that shoreline across the lake since I was a kid," Red Egan said. "Only George Crowder could know it better." Red grinned and added, " 'My Uncle George is the greatest fisherman in this town, county, or state!' "

"Come to think of it," Captain Lewis said, "I don't see why we have to wait till it is dark to go in there. Sheriff Egan and Crowder could drive right up to the front door of the Cogswell house, looking for a lost

41

boy in town, last seen in that area. They'll know it is a lie, but they'd have to respond. Meanwhile Egan and I can move in, openly, with some men and search the property from one end to the other. They can't go sniping at us if they are forewarned we're there."

"Let's go, George," Red Egan said.

Uncle George's Jeep took them quickly out of town to the Cogswell driveway. They turned in and the big stone house down by the lakefront came into view. A large American flag billowed from the rooftop, although it was long since time for it to have come down in the early evening shadow. There were a dozen other banners of some sort flying high. Uncle George slowed the Jeep as they started down toward the house. They could hear music that was being energetically played.

"Piano, saxophones, guitars," Uncle George said.

"Party?" Red Egan guessed.

"Or a regular life style. Joey has told me he could always hear music coming from there. Tried to persuade me to go with him to listen from a distance."

"You never went?"

Uncle George's smile was thin. "Waiting for an invitation," he said. "After all, I am a neighbor."

There was no sign of any local cars parked at the front of the house. They stopped the Jeep, got out and walked to the front door, and rang the doorbell. They couldn't hear it ring over the lively sounds of the music. But presently the door was opened from the inside by a black man wearing a white butler's jacket.

"I'm Red Egan, the sheriff of Lakeview. I'd like to talk to Miss Molly or Miss Polly, or both of them."

PATTERN FOR TERROR

"Care to state your business?" the butler asked.

"Whatever it is, it's none of yours," Red said. "Either of the Miss Cogswells, please."

Before the butler could reply, two rather gaudy women entered from a rear room where the music was the name of the game. Uncle George knew the Cogswell sisters by sight. One of them had hair as red as Red's. The other was a bright blonde. Each of them was wearing a skirt that ended before it reached the knees. Bright-colored blouses revealed more above the waist than would have been considered proper in Egan's world.

"What's wrong, Barton?" the red-haired one asked the butler.

"The local sheriff, Miss Dolly," the man replied.

"Don't shoot, Sheriff," Miss Dolly said, grinning at Red Egan.

"It's not a joke, Miss Cogswell," Red Egan said. "A local boy, ten years old, has turned up missing."

"You mean *not* turned up, missing."

Red nodded. "He was last seen in this part of the village. We thought he might have been attracted by your music. I've brought some men in to look for him. I wanted to warn you in case you and your friends spotted strangers outside your house."

"I suppose that is legal for you to do," Miss Dolly said.

"The boy has been missing since early this morning when he was seen just up the main highway from here. This is Mr. Crowder, the boy's uncle."

"Oh! Mr. Crowder is quite famous around these parts. They call you Uncle George, don't they, Mr. Crowder?"

"The boy we're looking for made him famous," Red said.

"I thought it was the wrong man who went to the gas chamber," Miss Dolly said.

"We just wanted you to know that we're searching your property for Joey Trimble," Red said. "We don't have to ask your permission. State troopers and deputies of mine are already at it. I'd like to ask your guests if any of them has seen a small boy with fair hair anywhere on the property or on the lake. I hope you won't object."

"Come into the next room," Miss Dolly said, turning her back and heading in the direction of the music.

"I ought to hire these people to play music for me," Uncle George muttered to Red Egan. "My favorite period!" He began to sing softly, " 'Somebody stole my gal, Somebody stole my pal . . .' "

The red-haired Miss Dolly led them into the room where the music was originating. There was a grand piano in the center of the room. An egg-bald man sat on the bench at the keyboard. There were seven or eight young men, all dressed in informal sports clothes, a couple of them with saxophones, a couple of guitarists, a banjo player, a drummer at a complicated set of drums, a trombonist. Uncle George was fascinated by the pianist. He was the famous Slick Evarts. If the others were in Evarts's class, the Cogswells had only the best.

Miss Dolly stopped by Slick and said she had to make an announcement. Evarts played an attention-getting set of chords on the piano and Miss Dolly held up her hands.

PATTERN FOR TERROR

"We have visitors!" she said. "This is Sheriff Egan of Lakeview, and Mr. Crowder who lives in the log cabin up off the main road. They're looking for a lost boy. Can you describe him again, Sheriff?"

"Ten years old," Red Egan said, "fair hair, wearing dark blue jeans, a bright red short-sleeved sports shirt, white tennis sneakers, and a white baseball cap with a dark blue visor."

The musicians looked around at one another. Uncle George didn't see a single face light up.

"The boy's name is Joey Trimble. His father owns the pharmacy in town. You might have seen Joey there. He was last seen this morning shortly after the tragedy on the main road up above you. You probably heard about it?"

"A teacher from the Academy dropped dead," Evarts said.

Uncle George nodded. "He and Joey were friends. Alex Francis comes back from a job in New York every Saturday morning—early bus. Joey saw him coming this morning. Francis waved to him and then toppled over into the ditch, dead."

"Heart attack, they said in town."

"It happened right near my cabin," Uncle George said. "We got help, took Francis to the emergency room at the hospital. Joey disappeared shortly after that."

"I don't know of any of us who've been in town this morning," Slick Evarts said. "You say the hospital is where he was last seen?"

"Yes."

Evarts seemed to relax. "You say you and the boy

45

have a collection of jazz records?" he said to Uncle George.

"Yes, and among them are two of yours, worn thin," Uncle George said.

"You play any instrument, Crowder?"

"A little piano, not under the same roof with you. A little guitar."

Evarts gestured to a guitar lying on the top of the piano. "Let's see if we can stir up something," he suggested, and sat down on the piano bench again.

Uncle George picked up the guitar and tested it for pitch. It was perfect. He looked up at the ceiling. If Joey could hear this, it might loosen some of the tension that he was feeling. Uncle George began to play the Robinson Crusoe song.

The other musicians joined in with saxes, trombone, guitars, drums. Uncle George had to admit it was exciting. When they swung around to play a second chorus, no one could sit still. When the second round was finished, the players applauded.

"We're here every Saturday and Sunday," Slick Evarts said. "You're good enough to join us anytime you feel like, George."

"Thanks so much," Uncle George said.

The door at the back of the music room opened and Miss Dolly Cogswell reappeared. With her were Sergeant Styles of the state police and Captain Lewis from New York.

Slick Evarts stood up, and brought his hand down in a flat-handed discord on the piano keyboard.

"So what has all this got to do with drugs?" he asked, his voice angry.

"What are you talking about, Slick?" Uncle George asked.

"Ask your friend there—Captain Lewis. I know him from way back."

"Hello, Slick," the captain said.

"You still playing the old double game, eh, Lewis? A lost boy? Which one of us are you really gunning for?"

Uncle George raised his hands, palms up, to Captain Lewis. It was a sort of helpless unasked question gesture.

Lewis nodded. There was no point in keeping the drug part of the Francis story a secret any longer.

"There is a lost boy, Slick," Uncle George said. "He is worse than lost. He's being held hostage to force us to back off a drug investigation."

"I'm sure of the drug part of that," Lewis said.

"It has to do with Alexander Francis who died on the highway earlier this morning. He didn't die of a heart attack," Uncle George said. "He was carrying heroin in a plastic container in his stomach. The container ruptured and he died of a massive overdose of the drug. He was carrying or delivering for someone."

"The old condom routine," Lewis said.

"Something very much like it. But we're not here because of any clue or solid evidence that leads to the Cogswell estate. It's more like a joke."

"I'm not laughing," Slick said.

"Joey and I were playing your album one day, Slick. The Robinson Crusoe number. We'd improvised with it and then Joey wondered where Crusoe and Friday might go on Saturday night if they lived

47

in Lakeview. He suggested here, because there were always men in strange trimmin' and wild women!"

Dolly Cogswell pointed to her sister and then to herself. "Wild women, love! How do you like it?" They both laughed.

"When I got back from a quick trip to New York, there was a threatening note from Joey's kidnappers. If we were to keep Joey from being hurt we must back off the drug case. Later they put Joey on the phone to me to warn me to back off. Joey spoke three words to me. They were 'Friday on Saturday.' They thought he said 'Friday and Saturday' and was about to tell me what had happened. I knew better. He was trying to tell me where he was. The only Friday on Saturday we had anywhere near here was this estate."

"I don't know why," Slick said, "but I tend to accept your story. Maybe I'm just a sucker for an honest face."

Slick turned to Miss Dolly, the red-haired sister. "I suggest you let Mr. Crowder and his friends go over the house and grounds with a fine-tooth comb, Dolly—attic to cellar. You and I know there are no drugs or kidnapped kids here. Let them have a free search." He looked at Uncle George. "I trust my friends here all the way down the road. You would go for your kid, right?"

"Right."

"Someone not connected with Molly or Dolly could be hiding the boy somewhere on this estate. Your boy tells you where he is, but not who's with him. Someone can be using us and fooling a smart ten-year-old at the same time. What do you say, Dolly? Let 'em have the run of the place?" Slick asked.

PATTERN FOR TERROR

"Of course," the red-haired Cogswell woman said. "And we'll see to it they look in every closet, every bureau drawer. I'm that sure there isn't an ounce of drugs in this place, anywhere."

"You show them through the bedrooms, Dolly," Slick said. "Any of you guys mind?"

One of the saxophone players spoke. "But don't read my mail! That girl from Garden City—"

Everyone laughed. The girl from Garden City spelled comedy of some sort to all of them.

"Dolly, you take someone through the bedrooms," Slick said. "I'll take someone on a guided tour of the downstairs, the cellar and kitchen quarters. Molly, you can head a tour of the outside—gardener's quarters, garage, and the other outbuildings."

Sergeant Styles went upstairs with Miss Dolly. Red Egan and Captain Lewis went with Slick Evarts to cover the downstairs and basement areas. Uncle George found himself going with Miss Molly to the outside area. Experience told him that they were not likely to stumble on a supply of drugs on any quick look. They drew a blank in the stables where a half dozen handsome saddle horses were stalled. A garden crew lived in a small cottage south of the kitchen. They weren't welcomed by a couple of housewife types who took care of their men there. Miss Molly had to explain in detail. They had found nothing when they finished. Uncle George stood looking at a red brick and stone building down at the lake's edge.

"So let's tackle the boathouse," he said.

"That's not ours," Miss Molly said.

"Same brick and stone work as the house," Uncle George said.

"Not ours," Miss Molly said. "It belonged to the estate originally, but the first owners sold it to the Academy before we bought the place," Miss Molly said. "They never changed its appearance."

"Joey might not have known that if he found himself in a red brick and stone building," Uncle George said.

"We'll have to get permission from Joshua Willis, the headmaster," Miss Molly said.

"He is in on the Francis case," Uncle George said. "I'll risk not asking him."

They walked across to the big boathouse and let themselves in. It contained four racing sculls, a supply of oars, and a quantity of other boating equipment.

"And a telephone," Uncle George said. "This is where someone could have put Joey on the phone to me. His fingerprints could be on it."

"You have a way to match them?" the blonde girl asked.

"I can surely find copies of Joey's prints at his home," Uncle George said. He had walked over to the telephone, which was a wall set located by a window that looked over to the Cogswell property. "Too late I'm afraid," he said. "This has been wiped totally clean since the last time it was used. Not a print of any kind on it. They must have suspected we'd look here."

Miss Molly had picked up a wastebasket and was looking through its contents. "Anything casual your boy might have left behind him?" she asked. "Like a chewing gum wrapper, for instance." She held out a crumpled piece of paper to Uncle George. "Wrigley's?"

"Joey's favorite gum!" Uncle George said. "He *was*

here! He was looking out the window when they put him on the phone, and thought he was on your property, Molly."

"Let's see if there is anything else," Miss Molly said.

"They won't have been that careless," Uncle George said.

"Once careless, always careless," Miss Molly said.

They began to look for something, having no idea what it might be. Suddenly the front door to the boathouse opened and Joshua Willis, the bearded headmaster of the Academy, walked in, accompanied by a boy wearing a gray uniform. Uncle George had forgotten that the Academy was a military school. All the students would be wearing a gray uniform with black trim and insignia.

"Mr. Crowder!" the headmaster said. "This is Corporal Simms. He told me he saw someone go into the boathouse. You might at least have asked permission. We could have responded a little more violently than this."

"Saw us from where?" Uncle George asked.

"My room is in South Hall," the cadet said. "I was watching the sun go down when I saw you go into this boathouse. I knew you weren't anyone from the Academy. I thought the lady was Miss Cogswell, so I reported it to the headmaster."

"How long had you been watching the sunset?" Uncle George asked. "Did you see anyone else leave earlier? My ten-year-old nephew is missing, kidnapped."

"I don't suppose I had been watching five minutes," Simms said.

"Is it part of your routine to wipe the telephone clean of any fingerprints after you use it?" Uncle George asked.

"No, sir. I'm not out for crew. I don't know what the crew coach's rules are," Corporal Simms said.

"I'm pretty damn sure my nephew was held here," Uncle George said to Willis. "Better late than never, I'd like to ask your permission to search—the whole Academy."

"That will be quite a chore," the headmaster said. "Four hundred and fifty boys, their rooms and lockers."

"Four hundred and sixty-seven cadets," the cadet said. "I know, because I work in the adjutant's office. Then there are the faculty and the housekeeping help."

"Hunting for a supply of drugs shouldn't be too hopeful," Uncle George said. "But a ten-year-old boy—?"

"Changed into an Academy uniform, he would just look like part of the scenery," Joshua Willis said. "But, of course, search away. Simms will act as a guide for you. Anything more on Alex Francis?"

"This is all Alex Francis," Uncle George said.

It was getting well on into the darkness of night. From the boathouse window they could see hundreds of lights on the Academy grounds. It looked like a small city.

"I could put together a squad of searchers for you, Mr. Crowder. No group of boys would be likely to conspire to keep your nephew hidden," Joshua Willis said.

"I'd be grateful," Uncle George said.

Willis started to leave and he was met in the doorway by a youngish man; middle thirties, Uncle George thought.

"Mr. Clark—Miss Cogswell and Mr. Crowder," Willis said.

"Mr. Crowder is something of a legend in this town," Clark said. "Of course I've seen him often going to his cottage up the road."

"And you and your wife were close friends of Alexander Francis," Uncle George said.

"Very close," Clark said, "and we are in shock."

"I can understand that."

"My wife and I would take an oath on our Bible that Alex had nothing to do with drugs," Clark said.

"He had enough in his gut to flatten a battleship and kill him!" Uncle George said.

"Mr. Clark is our rowing coach," the headmaster said. "Maybe he can answer some of your questions, Crowder."

"Had you heard, Mr. Clark, that someone has abducted my ten-year-old nephew and threatened to harm him if we don't forget about the drug investigation?" Uncle George asked.

"No."

"Joey was allowed to call me, spoke three words they didn't like, and he was cut off. Earlier today. There is some evidence that he was held here, made his phone call from here," Uncle George said.

"Evidence?"

"A chewing gum wrapper in the wastebasket, and a completely wiped-clean telephone."

"Anyone could be chewing gum," Clark said. "It's not a drug, not against the rules."

"And the phone?" Uncle George asked.

"This boathouse is given a thorough cleaning every Saturday morning," Clark said. "About nine o'clock."

Uncle George frowned. "That was before Joey made his call to me."

"So maybe your nephew didn't phone from here," the headmaster said.

"Whether he phoned from here or not," Clark said, "it is certain he isn't being held here now. I doubt if the lockers are big enough to hide a ten-year-old. What time of day was he taken?"

"The last time he was seen was at the hospital emergency room where they took his and your friend, Mr. Francis. Mid-morning. I had gone to New York to make inquiries about Francis's Friday-night job there."

"David Ash?"

"Yes, and I brought Leona Boyd back here with me."

"Leona! What does she say about drugs?"

"A quote for you," Uncle George said: "No way.' And yet Francis was killed by drugs he had taken internally."

"It just doesn't make sense," Clark said.

"Despite what you and Miss Boyd know about Francis," Uncle George said, "there are other things that make us wonder. There are two situations here within shouting distance of each other, right along the road Francis walked every Saturday morning, that could be prime markets for drugs. Miss Cogswell's musicians, and the student body here at the Academy."

"And was Alex carrying a supply for one addict in

his stomach or for more? He couldn't get rich that way, could he? We can check out his bank."

"Are you suggesting Francis was carrying drugs for cadets here at the Academy?" the headmaster asked.

"Schools are a prime market," Uncle George said.

"And pop musicians, you said."

"True."

"Well I can assure you we have never had a whisper of that kind of problem here at the Academy," the headmaster said. "Not a whisper!"

"Miss Cogswell?" Uncle George asked.

"Nothing," the blonde Cogswell sister said. "I admit it wouldn't be a stunning surprise. But I can assure you there has been no gossip about it."

"So your nephew misled you," Clark said.

"Not intentionally," Uncle George said. His face was set in hard, straight lines. "Joey was trying to tell me where he was. 'Friday on Saturday.' He was certainly referring to the song, not the days. This building had to look to him like a part of the Cogswell property."

"And it once was," Molly Cogswell reminded him.

"So what's next?" Joshua Willis asked.

"Check my gun and make sure it is loaded," Uncle George said. "Because if I find Joey and he has been misused, I'm going to need it in working order."

"You would kill?" Joshua Willis asked.

"Without a moment's hesitation," Uncle George said.

Anger was a primary emotion stirring in Uncle George, but even deeper and more painful was his anxiety for the boy he loved, and a sensation of guilt and responsibility for what may have happened to him. He had let Joey stay involved by letting him go to the hospital and leaving him there while he made his trip to New York. He should have sent Joey home with orders to stay put. He had let himself believe that a ten-year-old boy would use adult caution in a dangerous situation.

He was standing outside the boathouse with Joshua Willis. Molly Cogswell had gone back to her residence across the way.

"I know how you are feeling," the headmaster said. "I run up against it all the time. Only I have an army of kids to worry about. If one of them gets in real trouble, I tend to blame myself for not having foreseen it."

"Not a comfortable feeling," Uncle George said. "Can I ask you a couple of questions, Willis?"

"Of course."

"It seems to me there's something a little queer about the Francis situation. A regular member of your faculty teaching a course in the Extension department at Columbia in New York."

"Just Friday nights," Willis said. "His day here is finished. He didn't have to be here until assembly after breakfast on Saturday."

"Were you doing him a special favor letting him earn an extra salary each week?"

"I was doing someone else a favor," Willis said. "Dave Ash, the head of the English department. Dave once taught for me at Mohegan, some ten years ago. Last fall I hired Alex Francis to teach French and Spanish here at the Academy. He speaks both languages fluently. 'Spoke' I guess I should say. He explained that he was teaching at Columbia Extension and he would have to break his contract there to take the job I was offering him. In the process it turned out his boss was my old friend Dave Ash. I called Dave on the phone and he was not anxious to let Francis go. He was teaching a course called English Is Our Language. The students were all foreign-born adults, trying to settle into our society. Because of his facility with French and Spanish, Alex Francis was not replaceable. 'One in a million,' Ash said. He would have to refund tuition to more than one hundred students if Francis left in midstream of the year. In the end, I suggested we could let Francis be available for a Friday night course. Most of the Extension courses are in the evening and it would work. Ash could supply his pupils with what they had paid for; I could do an old friend a favor; Francis could make himself a few extra dollars and acquire some pride in being so much in demand."

"And his routine?" Uncle George asked.

"He would leave here after the last class on Friday, and he chose to stay in New York all night. The morning bus back got him to town about seven. It wasn't convenient to send someone to pick him up because the Academy is just stirring then. He chose to walk from the bus terminal to the Academy unless it was storming, and then he would hire a local cab. Either way he would reach the Academy about ten minutes after we had started breakfast. He would walk into the dining hall, signal to me at the head table, and that was it. That was reporting home.

When he didn't show up this morning, it was the first and only time—"

"You had reason to wonder if he was in trouble?" Uncle George asked.

"I don't think I thought of real trouble," Willis said. "A missed bus—a highway accident. He should have phoned me if he was not going to make it. But I really didn't have time to stew over it. Sheriff Egan called me before I got into a state of any real concern. So what next, Mr. Crowder? Finding the boy is your main concern, not solving a murder case."

"The *only* thing," Uncle George said, "I've now got to report to his parents. Report nothing, which isn't going to be easy."

"Tell them that we will turn over every leaf on the property here," Willis said, "with several hundred pairs of willing hands to do the work."

"Thanks. They'll appreciate that."

"I suggest the Cogswell ladies will give their place an equally thorough going over."

Uncle George's face hardened. "Let me say to you, sir, that there are rarely two places so close together that could be such prime markets for drugs."

"Carried in plastic in a man's stomach?" Willis sounded outraged. "A mass market but not a mass delivery," he said. "Well, good luck, Mr. Crowder. I trust you find your nephew safe and sound."

Joshua Willis had not helped to cheer Uncle George in any way. If someone wanted to keep Joey hidden, there would have been plenty of time in which to stow him away. What could Joey possibly know that would make him so dangerous to someone? He was being used to turn Uncle George and Red Egan and the others off the Francis case. But what did they know, or have a lead to, that could place anyone in danger? Nothing.

The word was out. When Uncle George drove his Jeep into town, there was a small crowd of people gathered outside Hector Trimble's pharmacy. Uncle George was swarmed with questions about the Francis death and his missing nephew. He wasn't able to supply anything very satisfying. His main and most painful prospect was not to be able to supply Joey's mother with anything positive. He hadn't been able to touch the doorbell to the Trimble's apartment, which was over the pharmacy, when the door opened and he was confronted by his haggard sister. One look at him and she knew he was not the bearer of good tidings. She just stood aside and let him in.

"Nothing?" she asked.

He reached out and touched her cold hand. "Nothing at the Cogswells', nothing at the Academy," he said. "There are literally hundreds of people looking for him. So far, no luck."

"I wish I really understood why he has been taken," Esther said.

"To stop your hero here from nosing into someone else's business." Hector Trimble's angry voice came from just behind his wife.

Hector was a huge man, well over six feet and weighing about two hundred and fifty pounds. Heroic proportions but with a nasty disposition that didn't allow anyone to think of him in heroic terms. His chief bitterness was due in part to the fact both his wife and his young son saw George Crowder as twice the man they had in him. It was not a situation he felt he had to handle with charm.

"Come in, George, and tell us what you know," Esther said. She was a small dark woman with gentle blue eyes and a straight thin-lipped mouth that suggested she could produce courage if it was called for. It was called for now, Uncle George thought. She had made one big mistake in her life, and he was standing behind her now, glaring at Uncle George as if he was certain that George Crowder was responsible for whatever had happened to Joey. As a matter of fact, that was exactly what Hector Trimble was thinking.

"Pin as many medals on yourself as you must, George," Hector said, "but try to mix in a few facts."

"Facts about Joey just haven't come to light," Uncle George said. "He had seen his friend Mr. Francis fall into the ditch, dead. Joey described how Francis had waved and beckoned to him before he fell. Joey went into my cabin and called Dr. Potter, the State Police, and Red Egan."

"Another local hero," Hector said in a tone of disgust.

"They all came and they loaded Francis into an ambulance and headed for the hospital. It appeared the man had died of a heart attack. Joey asked if he could go to the hospital with me."

"And you let him!" Hector said.

"Why not? Francis was his friend. I thought he was entitled."

"You thought!"

"Well, what harm was there, Hector?" Esther asked.

"He would be home here now if George had used some common sense," Hector said.

"I couldn't see that there was any risk in his going with me," Uncle George said. "The hospital was safe enough. Police everywhere. He was shocked at seeing his friend die. He was, I thought, entitled to know the real cause."

"Of course," Esther said.

"The autopsy showed that Francis had been carrying drugs in a plastic pouch in his stomach. The pouch had broken open and an overdose of the drug was the cause of death."

"Another hero type gone sour," Hector said.

"You are not hurting Joey's feelings or mine, Hector," Uncle George said.

"Give the boy's mother some hope!" Hector said.

"The note I got suggested Joey would be in danger if we didn't stop the drug investigation," Uncle George said. "No way I could, Es. The federal drug force, the state police, and Red Egan were already at it. But there is one thought to hang on to. Harming Joey just for the pleasure of it won't do them any good. But if Captain Lewis, Sergeant Styles, or Red Egan should come up with a suspect in the drug dealing that involved Francis, they could offer Joey for that suspect. In other words, until the next demand is made, I think we can hope that Joey is alive and not too badly hurt."

"How to cheer a mother on the day her son may have been murdered," Hector said.

"I may have to show you how to shut up a loud-mouthed jerk, Hector," Uncle George said.

Hector took a step backward, his fists raised. "I've always dreamed you'd try, George," he said.

The doorbell rang and Esther moved quickly to open it. Anything to stop the battle royal that was threatening. It was Red Egan, carrying a brown paper bag in his hands.

"They told me outside you were here, George," Red said. "But I really wanted to see you, Esther. I'm afraid what I have won't make you happy." He opened the paper bag and took out of it a baseball cap with a dark blue visor. "Joey was wearing a cap like this when we last saw him, Esther. Harry Parker found it floating in the lake just offshore from the Cogswell property. I hoped you might be able to tell us for certain whether or not it's Joey's." He handed the cap to Esther.

She instantly looked inside it, and from the stricken look that crossed her face Uncle George knew the answer. It was Joey's.

"There was a rip in the lining. I mended it for Joey." She held out the cap and showed them. "No question this is Joey's. What does it mean, Red?"

"The ugly possibility that Joey was drowned in the lake," Egan said. "That George was right in thinking Joey was really trying to tell George where he was—the Cogswell estate."

Hector Trimble brushed past the others for the door. "Harry Parker is a diver. I'll have him search the lake where this was found." And he took off.

Red Egan took back the cap and put it in the paper bag. "Parker is already at it," he said, "but I had a question to ask you, George. Did you find anything at the boathouse?"

PATTERN FOR TERROR

"A moment of hope," Uncle George said, and he explained about the wiped telephone and the chewing gum wrapper.

"This might support that theory," Red Egan said, tapping the bag with the cap in it. "As you know, George, the water in the lake moves slowly from east to west. If Joey was dumped into the lake earlier in the day and the cap floated away, it would have floated downstream to where it was found, just off the Cogswell property. I think Parker should be doing his diving well upstream and that we should be more interested in the Academy than the Cogswell jazz group."

Part Two

4.

A COUNCIL OF WAR WAS HELD ON THE BACK PATIO OF the Cogswell house. Uncle George, Red Egan, Sergeant Styles, and Captain Lewis of the federal drug force were trying to put their investigation on some kind of certain course. They were watching a man in diver's gear working on a flat-bottomed boat out on the lake.

"Harry Parker has been sent a message to move his search farther up the lake by the Academy," Red Egan said.

"It's not many small towns you come to where you find a professional diver-in-residence," Lewis said.

"We are a water-oriented community," Uncle George said. "We have rich people who own yachts and special sports type boats in profusion. There are many water disasters—sinkings, valuables lost overboard. During the spring and summer months there

67

are calls for Harry Parker's services almost every day."

"Many rich people, you say." Lewis tugged at his lower lip. "We have been thinking about a mass market for Francis's drug trade. We have an army of jazz musicians and the academy with hundreds of teenagers. But we keep passing by one key fact. Francis wasn't carrying enough in his stomach wallet to supply either of those markets."

"Carrying for just one customer?" Uncle George asked.

"One customer at a time, at any rate. There were three or four normal doses in the folder that ruptured," Red Egan said.

"But if there was just one customer, why bother with a messenger?" Captain Lewis asked. "He could pick it up himself without involving anyone else."

"Perhaps not if he were working for the Academy," Uncle George said, "and every hour of his time is dictated by a rigid scholastic schedule."

"You are saying a man couldn't pick up a business envelope full of powder without giving himself away?" Lewis asked.

"He would have to leave the Academy and travel to get it somewhere else," Uncle George said.

"This way he would have had to pay Francis a handsome fee," Lewis said.

"If he wanted it badly enough," Uncle George said.

"So there is someone on the New York end or on the way back from there who provided Francis, who then brought it back here on Saturday morning and delivered it to the buyer here. The buyer stays unnoticed and in his regular place here," Red Egan said.

PATTERN FOR TERROR

"It would have to be the Academy, I say," Uncle George said. "He had passed the entrance to the Cogswells' when he was struck down. Going to the Academy was his normal destination. Not noticeable to anyone for him to go to the place where he was a teacher. Francis did nothing that would have attracted attention. Joey saw him every Saturday, talked with him, may have played some kind of games with him. Today, disaster struck him down, but not until it was clear he was following his regular routine."

"So let's spell it out," Sergeant Styles said. "Francis went to New York every Friday afternoon, Leona Boyd met him there and stayed with him, except for an hour of classroom teaching, until he headed home Saturday morning. But sometime, probably on the bus back to Lakeview, somebody handed him the drugs he was to carry. All he had to do was swallow a plastic package. He didn't have to make any great show of it. He teaches his class and spends the rest of the night with Leona, and takes the morning bus back to Lakeview. He walks home to the Academy, stopping on the way to pass the time of day with Joey. Back at the Academy he can upchuck the drugs in his own room, and deliver them to the buyer."

"Could your nephew have been part of the deal?" Captain Lewis asked. "Francis passes the drug to Joey when they meet and he delivers it to the buyer?"

"No way," Uncle George said. "Joey would have told me when he saw Francis die. He would have to have known what he was doing and he would have told me. Of that I'm certain. But I'm equally certain that the Academy is the center of the action, not the Cogswell place."

"In spite of Joey's message to you—'Friday on Saturday'?" Lewis asked.

"Joey would never try to throw me off the path," Uncle George said. "Francis's customer is at the Academy."

"And there are dozens of very rich parents of boys at the school who could very well be drug addicts," Styles said. "Some from out of town, some local."

"So we have a situation where there is a seller in New York, a messenger who makes the trip once a week, and a buyer here," Red Egan said.

"But the messenger can't tell us anything, a buyer can't talk and stay out of jail, and a youngster we care about is kidnapped to keep us from getting too warm," Uncle George said.

"The Clarks," Red Egan said, "were Francis's closest friends. Maybe they could be persuaded to give us information that might help. Francis, you could almost say by a carelessly wrapped package supplied by the seller in New York, lost his life."

Harry Parker, the diver, was rowing his flat-bottomed boat toward shore. The last of Saturday's daylight was almost gone. Any outdoor search for Joey or clues to his whereabouts were becoming just about useless until morning.

Red Egan and Uncle George intercepted Parker when he came ashore.

"Nothing to help you," the man said. "The bottom of the lake along this shoreline is a study in carelessness. The Academy kids and that jazz outfit, which constantly changes, don't care a damn about what becomes of simple possessions. There are watches down there, sweaters and swimsuit tops, stuff enough to set up a small clothing store along with knick-knacks. But I haven't got much to go on for you. Blue jeans, a dark blue short-sleeved sports shirt, a pair of white sneakers, you said. That baseball cap you have, was it his?"

"His mother says it is. A repair she made some time ago makes it certain," Uncle George said.

"Then we're not just wasting time," Parker said. "I'll get started as soon as there's daylight in the morning. I'll try to get some underwater lights shipped up from New York. They have them there at the harbor."

"No body, is the main thing," Uncle George said, his voice unsteady.

"That we can swear to," Parker said. "The cap tells us the boy was somewhere around here. We didn't need the pants, shirt, and the sneakers. I've covered every inch of the shoreline east of the Cogswells' to here. I'd say you could feel easier."

Uncle George shook his head, slowly. "There is no assurance we will find him all in one piece," he said. "These bastards won't stop at anything if they think it will work on us."

"Evidence that they have harmed Joey won't stop you or the rest of us from keeping after them," Red Egan said. "It will keep us at it twice as hard, I'd say."

"Wish you luck. See you around in the morning," Parker said and took off.

An inquiry at the nearest building located the Clarks

in their ground floor apartment of South Hall, across the parade ground from where they had been talking with Parker.

"I don't hope for much," Uncle George said. "These people will cover for Alex Francis all the way down the line."

"If they think there is anything to cover for," Red Egan said.

"A bellyful of drugs isn't worth covering?" Uncle George asked.

Mrs. Clark answered their knock on the door. Stanley Clark was sitting at the table in a dining alcove just behind her. He looked pale and tired.

"Come in, Sheriff!" he called out. "And Mr. Crowder."

Uncle George and Red Egan brought them up-to-date on Harry Parker's finding of the cap and the rest of his report.

"I wish there was some way we could help," Clark said. "I don't think Jane and I have ever laid eyes on the boy to know him. Alex spoke about him and their Saturday morning meetings, but we were never out on the grounds at that time of day. I have to oversee a breakfast table in the dining hall in the morning. Jane can have a little more time to take it easy."

"There may be a way you can help," Uncle George said. "It has to do with your friend, Alex Francis."

"God help him," Clark said.

"He was doing a favor for someone," Uncle George said. "He was carrying heroin to somone or for someone. His arrangement of classes—one in New York on Friday nights, and the others during the rest of the week here; someone had to be benefiting on the educational level, the Academy or the Columbia Extension."

"I'd say both," Clark said. "Extension was able to satisfy a class that was already underway, and the Academy was able to acquire an exceptional language teacher for a long future."

"But who gave ground to make the deal?" Uncle George persisted. "David Ash at Extension could have held Francis to his contract until the end of the year. Joshua Willis could have refused to hire him while he had another obligation."

"And it could work the way it was working and satisfy everyone," Clark said.

"People like Willis and Ash aren't likely to give ground to a competitor," Uncle George said.

"They were not competing," Clark said.

"For a teacher, they were," Uncle George said. "Ash could refuse to let someone who had a contract with him take a full-time job somewhere else. Willis, head of a prestigious boys' school, isn't likely to let one of his faculty teach somewhere else, but they both did just that. Was one of them a very good friend of Francis's?"

"I think Dave Ash might come closest to fitting that description," Clark said. "He and Alex both graduated from Columbia—in the same year. That's when I first knew Alex. I was in their class. Alex was hipped on education. His whole dream in life was to teach at a high-grade school. He didn't know Willis, I'm sure. But he applied for the language job that was open here. It was a credit he might need in the future, far more valuable than the Extension credit. I know he asked Ash to release him when Willis offered him the job. At first Ash wouldn't go along with it, but it was Willis who figured out a way it would work for both of them," Clark said.

"Willis wanted it?" Uncle George asked.

"You don't know how good a teacher Alex was. If Willis didn't accommodate him then, he might never add him to his faculty."

"You're telling me what I wanted to know," Uncle George said. "One other question. Were Willis and Ash friends from some other time?"

"I've never heard that they were," Clark said.

"You two guys aren't covering the main ground," Red Egan said. "Drugs! Francis was ferrying drugs for someone—certainly making a profit for himself."

"And it killed him," Clark said.

"But it wasn't meant to," Red Egan said. "He wasn't murdered. He was carrying a deadly poison in a dangerous way and it fouled out on him. Terrible bad luck for him and dangerously bad luck for the people who were paying him. The word 'drugs' would never have been mentioned if Francis hadn't had his disaster."

"I simply can't believe that of Alex," Mrs. Clark said. She had brought a pot of coffee and some mugs to the table. "Do help yourselves, gentlemen."

"There are grammar school kids around on our streets making two or three hundred dollars a day delivering vials of crack and marijuana for dealers. Francis could have been making a lot more than that for delivering high-grade heroin to someone," Uncle George said.

"Someone in our town!" Red Egan said. "He wasn't carrying it from here to somewhere else. If he was, he'd have had to keep it in his possession for a week before he went to New York again."

"Does it occur to any of you that Joshua Willis may not have hired Francis because he was such a good language teacher, but because he was willing to deliver drugs? That he agreed to the unusual teaching schedule not for educational reasons, but because it set up a delivery system that seemed impenetrable and safe?" Uncle George said.

"Mr. Willis?" Jane Clark said. "A proverbial tightwad."

"We may be talking about what seems like a lot of money to us," Red Egan said, "but we are talking about the going amounts in the trade. If Willis or anyone else was paying it, they weren't being milked. It costs a lot to finance an addiction to heroin."

"Does Willis come from a wealthy family?" Uncle George asked.

Clark shook his head. "I've never heard any talk about his family, or known him to be visited by anyone identified as family."

"That Cadillac he drives around in wasn't bought with peanut shells," Red Egan said.

"I just don't believe it," Jane Clark said. "You have said it could work the other way around. Ash could be the buyer?"

"But Francis didn't die on upper Broadway," Uncle George said. "He died here, delivering."

"But not necessarily to Willis," Clark said. "It could be someone else here at the school, someone in town.

Francis could be delivering to a kid here at the Academy who passed it on to his father or someone else in town. Another step in a complex parade."

"Could be," Uncle George said, "and that someone is threatening my Joey—damn him."

"Why would they pick on you, Mr. Crowder?" Jane Clark asked.

"Because when drugs were revealed to be at the core of it, the buyer knew I would be involved. I had been connected with the federals when I left town for a span. He'd know about everyone in the area connected with drugs. Everyone in town knows how close I am to Joey, how precious he is to me. ABC."

"Do you know offhand, Mr. Clark, where Alex Francis did his banking business?" Red Egan asked.

"Locally, I suppose. Lakeview Bank and Trust. He has written some checks for local faculty affairs, and as I recall they were on the local bank."

"Don't let that cheer you up, Red," Uncle George said. "He would bank his explainable salary checks here just for the convenience of it. But if he was banking large amounts for his drug activities, it wouldn't be here. There would be too much gossip about it. We are talking about thousands of dollars."

"Deposited in New York?" Red Egan suggested.

"Probably," Uncle George said. "He left here on a Friday afternoon bus—too late to bank when he arrived in New York. He left New York early in the morning on Saturday, and that was too early to do any banking business."

"The post office isn't out of business," Red Egan said.

"Maybe he gave his mail to Leona Boyd to handle for him," Clark suggested.

"No reason to. All he had to do in New York was stop at a corner mailbox or use a bank with an automatic teller. No one would notice or comment about it. I think we had better get back to that young lady." Uncle George turned to the Clarks. "Don't pass along this conversation to anyone," he said. "If it should turn out to be Willis, he'll be waiting for us, holding Joey by his short hairs."

"We're a great deal more concerned about Alex Francis's reputation than Willis's. I still don't believe it's the way you are guessing, Mr. Crowder. Alex cared for the kids he taught, cared for the whole educational process. He just wouldn't undermine it by involving himself in crime. It would have been against everything he cared seriously about," Stanley Clark said.

"Extra money never stopped anyone from improving a situation a man cared about," Red Egan said.

"At any rate, don't pass it along," Uncle George said.

"You have our promise," Clark said.

"I hope that promise means something," Red said as he and Uncle George walked away toward the Academy grounds.

"You think he may be involved?" Uncle George asked.

"No. But Willis may be his friend, and he is his boss. He may think that is where his loyalties should lie. So he may alert Willis to where you are headed, George."

"And Willis still has a weapon he can use against me," Uncle George said.

"Joey?" Red Egan asked.

"Joey. He has got me in a clamp no matter which way the chips fall."

"So, your next move?" Red asked.

"Willis—with not too much hope."

Darkness had overtaken the countryside. The two men were standing just inside the huge iron gates that marked the entrance to the Academy grounds and the handsome white colonial house where Joshua Willis lived.

"The school does nicely by its headmaster," Uncle George said.

The downstairs windows of the house and one or two rooms of the upper floor were lighted.

"He built it for himself when he bought the school," Red Egan said. "This was during the time when you were living away. I've heard he owns seventy-five percent of the school corporation stock."

"Not bought with peanut shells either," Uncle George said. "So he does have money."

"The only person who can fire Joshua Willis is Joshua Willis," Red said.

"Let's have a go at him," Uncle George said.

"If he has Joey?" Red asked.

"God help him and me," Uncle George said.

The front door to the Willis house was opened by another black man in a white servant's jacket. "Hello, Sheriff," the man said. "I think Mr. Willis is expecting you."

"We would like to see him. By the way, are you

related to the man who works for the Cogswells? You could be twins," Red said.

"He is my brother," the man said. "His name is Paul Barton. I'm Zach Barton. Zachery Barton."

"Will you announce us?" Uncle George asked.

"I was told to bring in the police when they came," Zach Barton said. "Mr. Willis is in his study. This way."

He led them across a wide hallway to a big door at the far end. Joshua Willis was seated at a handsome mahogany desk, surrounded by stacks of papers.

"Hello, Sheriff—Mr. Crowder. Come in. I was expecting Sergeant Styles. He has about twenty-five state policemen searching the dormitories and the faculty quarters for some evidence of drugs. I suspected I was to be next. Any sign of your nephew, Mr. Crowder?"

"None, I'm sorry to say."

"There isn't any way he could be safely hidden here at the Academy. Every inch of the place is being covered by the students and the faculty with orders to look for him—plus Sergeant Styles' army of state police and FBI men. But if you are here to search for him, help yourselves. That far door leads to my personal quarters. Barton can take you on a tour. Are you still convinced, Mr. Crowder, that Alex Francis was carrying drugs for my school?"

"A little less convinced that I can prove it," Uncle George said. "A man who is as ready as you are to let his place be searched must feel certain that nothing will be found that can incriminate him. As you say, Sergeant Styles has special techniques for drug hunting. I'll leave that to him."

"It will take him all night to cover the school," Willis said.

"I'm much more concerned about my nephew. He mustn't be subjected to violence all night."

"I sympathize with you. A traumatic experience for a ten-year-old."

Uncle George and Red Egan thanked the headmaster and left. In Uncle George's Jeep they headed back toward town. Uncle George felt he should check with his sister again. The monsters who had Joey might start threatening her.

About a half mile down the road, Red Egan pointed.

"The light outside the front door of your cabin is on, George. Could someone be there, or left more notes?"

Uncle George spun the Jeep's wheel and headed down his own driveway. The headlights picked up the answer to Red's question. A small body was stretched out on the stone step outside the door. In the terrible moment of first seeing it, Uncle George didn't have to be told who it was.

"It's the boy!" Red said.

The Jeep skidded to a stop and both men jumped out and ran.

Joey was lying on his back on the wide stone slab. There was blood everywhere, coming from a terribly battered head, and from four or five stab wounds in his chest. The handle of a kitchen carving knife protruded from one chest wound.

"Jesus, George!" Red Egan said.

Uncle George bent down and lifted the boy. Blood drained all over his shirt and jacket.

PATTERN FOR TERROR

"I can't tell that he's breathing," Uncle George said. His voice broke. "I can't detect a pulse."

Red Egan had gone into the cottage to the phone.

Uncle George cradled the boy, speaking softly. "Joey, Joey, Joey."

Red came out of the cabin. "Doc Potter and an ambulance are on the way. Anything, George?"

"No, God help us," Uncle George said.

Part Three

5.

WAITING FOR THE AMBULANCE AND RIDING IN IT WITH
Joey to the hospital was perhaps the most painful
experience Uncle George could remember. Dr. Potter
didn't come in the ambulance. He was waiting in the
emergency room when they got to the hospital. Uncle George had had enough experience with first aid
at fires, car accidents, and drownings in the lake to
know that at the very best it was touch-and-go for
Joey. How long he had been suffering the profuse
bleeding from his head and chest wounds was an
unknown. There was a lot of blood on the stone step
outside Uncle George's door, but no indication that
the attack on Joey had taken place there. The boy
could have lost several pints of blood before he was
deposited where they had found him. It could well
be too late for help.

Red Egan had taken off in the Jeep to find Sergeant Styles and notify the state police. It might be

85

quicker to get to him at the Academy or the Cogswells' wherever he was, than to leave a phone message for him at headquarters, though that was done, too.

The young medic who came in the ambulance was pretty grim at what he found.

"Oxygen and surgery may give him a chance," he said.

"May?" Uncle George asked.

"I'm afraid it is that bad, Mr. Crowder."

Uncle George held the boy close, saying his name over and over. Courage might give the boy a chance, too. If he could hear his beloved uncle's voice, it might act as a shot in the arm. But there was no sign that the boy heard anything.

Dr. Potter was waiting at the emergency room and Joey was whisked away. Then Uncle George went through the painful business of notifying Esther and her husband. Uncle George could hear Hector roaring in the background, as he tried to warn Esther how bad things looked. Half an hour later the frightened couple joined Uncle George at the hospital. Hector was armed with a double-barreled shotgun.

"I should have known that sooner or later you would lead Joey into fatal trouble," Hector announced.

"He wasn't with me when he was taken hostage," Uncle George said. "If he had been, you know damn well it could never have happened, Hector."

"I wonder how you'll be able to live with it," Hector said.

Uncle George wondered the same thing. He had left Joey here at the hospital when he returned to New York to find David Ash, Alex Francis's boss, and came back with Leona Boyd, Alex's girl. He should

have given Joey a strong warning to stay put. He had
been sure the boy would respond to the situation in
an adult fashion. That was expecting too much of a
ten-year-old whose only purpose in life would have
been to be useful to his adored uncle and hero.

Only the cool feel of Esther's hand on his made the
slowly passing time bearable.

It was eventually past midnight when Dr. Potter,
wearing his surgical gown, emerged from the next
room. He looked far from reassuring.

"George. Esther," he said. He nodded to Hector
without mentioning his name. "I'm afraid I can't
offer much cheer."

"Not—?" Esther murmured.

"Joey's alive," the doctor said, "but I can't promise for how long. The wounds to his head are severe.
Multiple skull fractures, severe bleeding. The chest
wounds are very, very bad. I can do what must be
done to care for them. I've been in touch with Dr.
Linder in Hartford, a brain specialist. He is on his
way, and should be here in about an hour. He is the
best."

"Thank you, Doctor," Esther said. "Joey hasn't
been able to speak?"

"No. And with the best of luck, it may be days
before he can. And he may never remember what
happened to him. He might not even remember who
you, or his father, or George are."

"Oh, God!" Esther said.

"Nothing to lead us anywhere?" Hector asked, running his hand along the barrel of his shotgun.

"Guesswork," Dr. Potter said. "There are a couple
of splinters of wood in the head wounds. There is

so much on television and the radio about gang fighters using baseball bats to hurt people, and it is the same kind of wound. But there are hundreds of baseball bats available at the Academy."

"With bloodstains and fingerprints on them?" Hector asked.

"A bat that could be identified that way could long since have been thrown in the lake, or tossed from a speeding car miles from town. And, there are a lot of kids in town who don't go to the Academy and who have bats."

"I remember delivering a medical order to the Cogswell house a week or so ago," Hector said. "They have a softball diamond out back. I remember seeing a rack with a dozen or more bats on it."

"I think you can be sure if a bat was used to inflict those terrible wounds to Joey's head, you won't find it just lying around," Dr. Potter said.

"The knife?" Uncle George asked.

"An ordinary kitchen carver," the doctor said. "One in every household for carving beef, lamb, pork, chicken."

"Fingerprints?" Hector asked.

"They were washed off the blade by Joey's blood. I'm afraid the only prints on the handle will be George's from when he removed the knife from Joey's chest."

Hector's laugh was bitter. " 'My Uncle George is the greatest detective in this town, this state, this nation.' How absurd can you get?"

Uncle George could hear Joey speaking those words with pride. "The grestest detective in this town, this county, this state, this nation." Hector had left out the county.

There was nothing to do but sit here with the cool of Esther's hand on his, the irritation of Hector's contempt nibbling at him, and the suspense of waiting for what might next come from the doctor. The truth of the matter was that he hadn't backed off after the first warning, and it had cost Joey dearly. But he might as well have backed off because he had come up with nothing. Back off from what? The drug case? He wasn't any closer to an answer to that situation than he had been when he had pulled Alex Francis out of the ditch that morning. That morning? It seemed like a year ago! A suspicion or two, one suggested by Joey which had sent him without results to the Cogswell house and the boathouse, but nothing to suggest that the violent attack on the boy had taken place there.

"You are just letting him bleed to death while we wait for your doctor from Hartford?" Hector asked.

"I've managed to pretty well stop the chest bleeding," Dr. Potter said. "The head wounds are the most dangerous. Dr. Linder will have to handle those."

"The late Dr. Linder," Hector said.

"We would all do better without your sour comments, Hector," Dr. Potter said.

"That's my kid in there!"

"And Esther's, and George's in a way," the doctor said.

"That's what may cost him his life, trying to be George's kid!"

A nurse came in the waiting room. "There are people outside with questions about the boy," she said. "Most of them are asking for Mr. Crowder."

"He's the right person to ask what happened to Joey," Hector said. "What happened is his fault."

Uncle George followed the nurse out of the room, and went to the door she indicated. He found himself standing on a small platform or landing atop a short flight of stairs that led down into a sort of meeting room. The floor of that room was cluttered with folding chairs, thrown about indiscriminately. At the far end of the room three people sat together. Uncle George had no difficulty identifying them, even at that distance. They were Joshua Willis, the bearded headmaster at the Academy; Miss Leona Boyd, Alex Francis's attractive girl friend; and Slick Evarts, the bald jazz pianist, a member of the Cogswell sisters' entourage.

"There were more than a hundred people here," the nurse said, "yelling, shouting, playing games with the folding chairs, getting into places they were not supposed to be. The hospital brass ordered them to wait for you out in the parking lot beyond that far door. It's a beautiful day so that was not a hardship."

"But those three didn't go?"

The nurse's face hardened. "Joshua Willis has three or four hundred young boys in his care eight months of the year, playing baseball, football, hockey, skiing. They get hurt. Willis may be the hospital's best customer. He is also one of the top stockholders in the corporation that runs the hospital. You don't say no to Joshua Willis around here. He brought the woman with him."

"And Slick Evarts?" Uncle George asked.

The nurse's face relaxed. "Slick has provided the patients and the staff of this hospital with delightful entertainment. It wasn't difficult to make a special dispensation in his case."

The people under discussion had spotted Uncle George and were coming toward him, fighting their way through the mess of chairs. Uncle George went down to greet them.

"Crowder," Willis said, "you can't know how bad we feel about the news of your nephew. We know how you must be hurting. We all came here, we and your friends outside, in the hope that we could offer you some kind of help."

"Help with what?" Uncle George asked.

"You have two murders to solve—Alex's and your nephew's."

"The boy isn't dead," Uncle George said.

"But we heard of the terrible injuries! No chance, we heard. I've had some experience with violence, not criminal, but in the line of sports. The best man anywhere regarding head injuries is a Dr. Albert E. Linder in Hartford. I thought I might persuade him to come and look at the boy."

"Dr. Linder is on his way," Uncle George said.

"Then the boy *will* live. Has he told you who abducted him and beat him so brutally?" Willis asked.

"He hasn't told us anything and he may never tell us anything even if he lives," Uncle George said.

"So you are still at square one," Willis said.

"Where I would have been if I had backed off," Uncle George said.

He turned to Leona Boyd. "Your reason for staying to see me, Leona?" he asked. "In what way did you think you could help me?"

"I'm afraid my reasons for staying weren't as unselfish as Mr. Willis's," the girl said. "I stayed because I thought you could help me. My man, Alex Francis, could no more have been involved in the drug traffic, or taking drugs, than the man in the moon! You say he couldn't have swallowed that heroin by accident. I say it is the only way he could have done it. I knew that man so well, Mr. Crowder. Circumstances permitting, we lived together around-the-clock, hour after hour, day after day. He couldn't have been involved with drugs in any way without my knowing about it."

"You hadn't been living around-the-clock with him lately," Uncle George said, "not since he has been teaching here at the Academy."

"That didn't make me know him any less well," the girl said.

"The doctors say he couldn't have swallowed the dose that killed him by accident," Uncle George said.

"Larger than a big hot dog," Joshua Willis said. "He would have to practice to manage that."

"So he thought he was carrying a breakfast treat for someone," the girl said.

"That much trouble every Friday?" Uncle George asked.

"Not if it was for a good friend."

"Who?"

"I don't know. The Clarks, maybe."

"According to our FBI expert, what was found in Francis's stomach had a street value of twenty-five to thirty thousand dollars. The fee for delivery is usually ten percent of the street value," Uncle George said. "Twenty-five hundred to three thousand dollars a week would be a handsome addition to a school teacher's salary."

"Not Alex," the girl said. "Not ever! His moral code would not have let him. If he was carrying something in his stomach, knowingly, someone bamboozled him into it!"

"Why would a breakfast treat be carried so secretly?" Uncle George asked. "No one would have searched him for a cinnamon bun, and if they had, it wouldn't have mattered. There wouldn't have been anything criminal about it. The man was ferrying drugs, carrying them in a way they wouldn't be found if he was stopped and searched."

"I'm telling you Alex would never have—"

"I'm sorry I don't believe you," Uncle George interrupted. "Francis would be proud and pleased to hear how much you trusted him, and perhaps a little shamefaced to know that he didn't deserve that trust."

"Maybe you and I should go to the Clarks and talk," Willis said to the girl. "You haven't spent a lot of time with Alex for the past months—since he took on the double teaching job here and at Columbia. He spent a lot of time with the Clarks and he might have confided in them."

"I suppose it is worth a try," the girl said.

Uncle George and Slick Evarts watched the girl and the headmaster go to the exit. They could hear the rumble of the voices in the parking lot, as the door opened and closed.

"Men dream of having women with that kind of faith in them," Evarts said.

"If it is justified," Uncle George said. "How did you imagine that you could help me, Slick?"

"You were pointed to the Cogswell estate," Slick said. "You reminded me of the old Robinson Crusoe song. The boy's phone call, it was 'Friday on Saturday,' wasn't it—not Friday and Saturday?"

Uncle George nodded.

"If you want something at the Cogswells', if you want to quiz anyone, if you want drug tests, I can get it for you. I can get anything you want there."

"Why would you?" Uncle George asked.

"The boy liked my music, so I like the boy. But you have troubles, George. When it becomes generally known that the boy didn't die, the bastard who beat him will have a second try. Or as soon as your Joey can remember and talk, that character's goose is cooked. He isn't going to wait for that to happen."

"Only hospital people will be with Joey. They can be trusted I think," Uncle George said.

"A world of faith!" Evarts said. "The Boyd girl for her man, you for a hospital nurse. Who could keep the name of the murderer to himself or herself?"

"There has been no murder."

"Not Francis," Slick said. "But your boy was meant to die, and there will be another try at him when it is known he may soon be able to talk. You had better set up barricades, George."

Uncle George looked up at the ceiling. Above it he knew Joey was fighting for his life. Uncle George knew he should be up there waiting for Dr. Linder to arrive and make a prognosis after he had examined the boy.

"One more thing, George," Slick Evarts said. "I know you are not a country bumpkin. You were once the smartest prosecuting attorney in these parts. You retired when you convicted an innocent man on false evidence provided by the state police."

PATTERN FOR TERROR

"So an innocent man died in the gas chamber."

"Not your fault. You should trust your instincts as a crime fighter. They took you to the Cogswells'. A group of vacationing jazz musicians are bound to include drug users. You were right. Personally, I smoke about six joints a day. There are others who take a short shot of other stuff— cocaine, heroin. But there is one thing about all of us, George: we are all out of work for reasons of health, the end of a tour, and in my case the failure of a record company. Not one of us could possibly make a twenty-five-thousand-dollar buy. Not every week, not once in a coon's age. None of us could have paid for Alex Francis's services. You can drug-test us all and we'll look bad. But we simply couldn't have been involved with Francis's kind of deal. So, check us out. Most of us are on drugs. If Joey found us out, there's no reason to try to stop him from talking. Nothing can be proved against us."

"I had better check on my friends out in the parking lot," Uncle George said. He walked out the far door to the lot. They were there as the nurse had said—an army! Loud shouts went up as Uncle George appeared.

"How is he, George?"

"Is the boy still alive?"

Uncle George waved his arms for silence. "Joey is still alive," he called out. "But he can't talk. There is something you people can do to help, though."

"Name it, George!"

"Joey wasn't attacked at my place where we found him. It must have happened somewhere between the Academy and the Cogswells'—or the woods in back of my place. If we could find the place where it happened, it might point to something or someone. There may not be too much mess, except blood. It wouldn't take too much effort for a grown man to subdue a ten-year-old boy."

"A crazy man!" someone suggested.

"Yeah! Only a crazy man would have to give the kid such a beating."

"If you guys could look for the place, it may help us," Uncle George said.

They all took off, some going to their cars, others running on foot to the gates. Exit the army.

Uncle George watched them go and then went back into the hospital. He crossed the big inside hall. Slick Evarts was gone. Uncle George climbed the short flight of stairs to the waiting room. The nurse who had helped him before was still there.

"Dr. Linder is here," she told him.

"I need to talk to him when he is free," Uncle George said.

"He is looking for you," the nurse said. "He should be here any minute. I was going to take him down to the parking lot where I thought you might be."

"How is Joey?"

"The same. But you may be able to help. He's lost a large amount of blood and neither his mother nor father can give blood just now for a transfusion. They hoped that you, his only other living relative, might fill the bill."

"Anything for Joey," Uncle George said.

The door at the end of the room opened and a man came in. He was middle-aged, Uncle George guessed, though his hair was snow-white. It was close-cropped like a young athlete's hair. Very bright blue eyes looked out from behind shell-rimmed glasses.

"This is Mr. Crowder, Doctor," the nurse said. "Mr. Crowder, Dr. Linder."

"The nurse has explained to you about your nephew's condition, Mr. Crowder?" the doctor asked.

"Of course I'll do anything I can," Uncle George said.

"You know your blood type?"

"No."

"Come with me and we will check it out," Dr. Linder said, leading the way. "If you will wait a few minutes, Mr. Crowder, I'll get a nurse to draw a sample."

"What are Joey's chances?"

"Not great. He should have been dead. He was left for dead or certain to die where you found him on your front doorstep. Something of a miracle."

"Miracle?"

"It turned out to be not exactly as it was explained to me on the telephone," the doctor said. "He was struck on the head fifteen or twenty times, but not with some heavy weapon like a baseball bat. More like a switch, back and forth. His scalp is badly lacerated, but X-rays don't show any major internal damage to the skull, except for bleeding, which could damage his brain function. The miracle is that five stab wounds to the chest didn't touch his heart or any other vital organ. Again, massive bleeding."

A nurse approached, bent over Uncle George and took a sample of blood from his forearm.

"Let us pray," Dr. Linder said.

"Are you a religious man, Doctor?" Uncle George asked.

"I wish I were. I need to see things more clearly than I do. I have a picture of a man, striking the boy on his head with some sort of nonlethal weapon, and stabbing him with a knife held in his other hand. A wild attack for a grown man on a small boy, especially if all that was needed was to kill him. It suggests something else to me."

"Oh?"

"That it might have been two people!" Dr. Linder said.

The nurse came back carrying a small slip of paper that she handed to the doctor. She was smiling.

"Thank God," Dr. Linder said, and then to Uncle George, "you're it, Crowder. Maybe I should keep praying. It seems to work. Now we pray that it will be in time!"

The boy lay on a bed in the operating room of the hospital, his head swathed in bandages, absorbent patches taped to his chest. His parents sat beside him, Esther holding his hand. Hector still holding his shotgun.

"It had to be you!" Hector said.

Uncle George felt a fierce anger sweep over him. "You'd rather Joey die than I help him to live?"

"George! Thank you, thank you," Esther said.

"Just a lucky chance," Hector said. "He was born lucky."

Dr. Potter had joined them and he and Dr. Linder went about the business of preparing for the transfusion.

"No word from him about who was responsible?" Uncle George asked.

"No word from him of any kind," Dr. Potter said.

"We will have to stay lucky if he ever talks to us again."

How much longer it was Uncle George didn't know, but he found himself lying on a cot beside Joey's bed, feeling weak and a little dizzy. He had given what he could of his own substance to the boy.

"When will you know if it works?" he asked.

"It will be a while," Dr. Potter said. "You have done all you can do, George. Are you able to talk to Sergeant Styles? He is waiting outside for you."

"Can you wheel me to him? I don't feel—"

"Of course."

Sergeant Styles was waiting in the next room. "We just have to hope our luck holds out," he said, as Uncle George was brought to him. "Dr. Linder has told you about his theory that it might have been two people who attacked Joey?"

"Make sense to you?" Uncle George asked.

"It could have been a couple of those crazy, drug-loaded jazz musicians at the Cogswells'," Styles said.

"Or kids from the Academy," Uncle George said.

"We have come up with something I guess you don't know about yet," Styles said. "The examination of Francis's body shows there was a second package of drugs in his gut, undamaged. That guy was carrying heroin with a street value of close to thirty thousand dollars. The girl insists he must have swallowed the one that killed him by accident. But two, never! This was big-time stuff handled by experts, that misfired. If the boy found out or guessed who they are, he couldn't be allowed to live."

"But if he tells us what he knows, will it be evidence?" Uncle George asked.

"There is a lot of talk about prayer around here," Styles said. "I join in."

It was the longest twenty-four hours Uncle George could remember. He glanced at his watch. It was Sunday afternoon! It was more than twenty-four hours. It had started at seven o'clock Saturday. He was finishing his breakfast coffee when he heard Joey calling him. The boy had just seen his friend Alexander Francis topple into a roadside ditch dead! They had gotten the body to the hospital where an autopsy revealed Francis had been ferrying drugs. Uncle George had been deputized by the sheriff to help track down the person who might be Francis's buyer. The middle part of the day had been taken up by the drive to New York to interview David Ash, Francis's employer at Columbia. That had led him to Leona Boyd, Francis's grief-stricken girlfriend, who had come back to Lakeview with him. Then the warning. "Back off—or else." Back off from what? They didn't have the slightest lead to anything. Then the phone call from Joey and the three words spoken in a frightened voice—"Friday on Saturday"—which Uncle George took to be a clue based on an old private joke. "That island with cannibal trimmin', Where there are wild men There must be wild women." These lyrics from an old song which Joey had thought suggested the Cogswells, if Friday and Crusoe had been living in Lakeview. But an inquiry and search there had produced no trace of the boy. It was after nightfall when Uncle George and Red Egan had found the boy, brutally beaten and stabbed, lying on the front steps of Uncle George's cottage in the woods. From then on the only concern was to save

Joey's life. That had led, finally, to the transfusion, which left Uncle George woozy and unsteady on his feet.

"Is there anything you can give me that will renew my energy?" he asked Dr. Potter.

"The only thing that will renew your energy, George, is some sleep. You have been at it for hours. You won't be able to do anything for Joey now, so go home and get some sleep. We'll let you know if there are any vital changes in Joey's condition."

Red Egan volunteered to drive Uncle George home in the old white Jeep.

"Call me in a couple of hours," Uncle George said as they pulled up to the cottage.

"You need more than that," Red said. "I'll come for you Monday morning."

Uncle George staggered into the cottage, went to the bedroom at the rear, slipped out of his clothes and crawled into bed. He must have been sound asleep before his head hit the pillow.

He had no idea how much later it was when he woke. He was choking and coughing, and as he pushed himself up on his elbows, he realized that the room was thick with smoke. Fire! He got up and went to the bedroom door. The front of the house was a mass of flames. He had to get out of there. No time to dress. He found an old bathrobe hanging on the closet door, slipped into it, and went to the window next to the bed. He tried to open the lower frame, but it was swollen shut by summer humidity.

He picked up a small, upright chair beside the bed and smashed out the window. Strangling from the smoke, he crawled out through the broken window and dropped into the flowerbed below. He started to rise when he felt a sudden sharp pain at the top of his left shoulder. He reached up to touch it and his hand came away bloody. He was experienced enough to know that he had been shot. If he stood up and tried to walk away, he would be an easy target for the gunman.

Then he heard someone calling to him. It was Red Egan coming around from the front of the house.

"George! For God's sake, George!"

Uncle George stayed where he was. If he stood up, he would be a perfect target. Red came close to the smashed window and Uncle George reached out and grabbed his leg.

"George!"

"Someone is shooting at me."

"Stay put. I'll go around to the front and get the Jeep."

"So you became a target, too?"

Red Egan's face was grim. He reached in his jacket pocket and brought out a .45 caliber handgun.

"If I do," he said, "it will become tit for tat."

Part Four

6.

UNCLE GEORGE, HUDDLED IN THE FLOWERBED, GLANCED around. Flames were pouring out the window through which he had just escaped. The whole interior of the cottage was on fire now, and very presently the outside of the house would go, too. He couldn't stay where he was. But if he moved, the gunman might take a second shot at him. Still, there was no choice.

He crawled a few yards away from the house, waiting for the sound of a gunshot and the sharp pain of a bullet. Nothing. And then Red Egan came back from the front of the cottage, driving the Jeep. He pulled up beside Uncle George.

"Nobody in sight out front," he said.

"Guy probably thought he got me," Uncle George said.

"Get in and stay crouched down," Red said. "You didn't call the fire department, did you?"

"No time."

"We'll stop at the Cogswells' and call from there," Red said.

"It's too late to save the cottage. All my clothes are gone and my prized possessions from years back," Uncle George said.

They drove away, heading across the highway to the Cogswells'. The two women, Dolly and Molly, were standing out front, staring at the smoke that was pouring up from the cottage.

"Thank goodness you are all right, Mr. Crowder," Molly said as the two men pulled up.

"May I use your phone to call the fire company?" Red asked.

"We have already called them," Dolly said. She turned her head, listening. They all heard it—the sound of the siren on the fire truck as it raced down the highway toward the burning cottage.

"I was asleep," Uncle George said. "Just made it out."

"Oh, wow," Molly said.

And then Slick Evarts appeared from around the back of the house. He had a rifle tucked under his right arm.

"All's well," he said to the girls. Then to Red and Uncle George, "A fox was molesting our cat. I got him. Fire looks bad."

"Total," Uncle George said.

"You shot a fox?" Red asked. He and Uncle George were thinking the same thing. Could it have been Slick who fired at Uncle George?

"Let me see that gun," Red said. He didn't wait for it to be handed to him. He literally wrenched it away from Slick. "Somebody shot George in the shoulder!"

Slick laughed. "You're not suggesting that I—?"

"This gun has been fired twice," Red said.

"I fired twice at Br'er Fox," Slick said. "Missed him the first time. Got him right in the head the second time. You'll find him in the trash pail out back, if you care."

"I'll keep the gun," Red said. "If we can find the bullet that was fired at George, it may be important to us. And to you, Evarts, if this is or isn't the gun that was fired at George."

"There are probably better ways to waste your time," Slick said. "Why on earth would I try to shoot Mr. Crowder?"

"Because you thought he was getting too close to the truth."

"And because if you are responsible for what happened to Joey," Uncle George said, "you know I wouldn't wait for the law to deal with you."

"This is all absurd," Molly Cogswell said. "Are you still thinking that we were involved in Alex Francis's drug game? Search the place again! Search all of us!"

Another car drove up to the house. In it were Captain Lewis and Sergeant Styles of the state police.

"We thought we might find you here," Lewis said to Uncle George. "These ladies called the fire department and they also called us."

"Why the police?" Uncle George asked the women.

"That fire had to be a crime," Dolly Cogswell said. "And if you were there—"

"Well, I was, as you know, Captain. But I was lucky enough to make it out alive."

"Any notions? Did you hear anyone torching the place?"

"No. But it certainly was done after I got there. There was no fire when I crawled into bed." He went on to tell how he got out and the shot that had knicked him in the shoulder.

"Bastard is determined," Lewis said.

"He's destroyed everything I own, but not me yet," Uncle George said.

"So we keep you somewhere safe till we catch him," Lewis said.

"No way," Uncle George said, "not while he will be trying to keep Joey from telling us what he knows. I'll buy myself some clothes and stay right on it with you."

Another car came up the driveway toward them. Uncle George knew the driver. He was Jerry Byers, one of the friends who had been waiting in the parking lot and had set out to try to find the scene of the crime.

"We think we found it, George!" Byers called out.

"Where?"

"On the lakefront," Byers said. "South of here. About twenty yards from the Academy property, on your side, Miss Cogswell."

"What makes you think—?" Lewis asked.

"It's muddy there," Byers said. "Signs of a struggle. Blood. Footprints. A set of a heavy man's prints, and"—Byers glanced at the Cogswell sisters—"a woman's."

Slick Evarts smiled. "Let's go have a look and you can see whether my shoes fit the man's prints."

"Not the shoes you are wearing," Byers said. "You have on tennis shoes. The prints out there were made by a heavy set of shoes, with square leather heels."

"Well, look up in my room and see if I have a pair of shoes that will match," Evarts said.

He was, Uncle George thought, taking pleasure in being suspected of something he hadn't done, or he was a good enough actor to get them to think that was what he was doing.

They all started down across the wide lawns to the place where a couple of Byers's friends were waiting.

"I almost walked right over it before I spotted it," Byers said. "You can read it like a book."

The week's earlier rain had left the lakeside soft and almost wet underfoot. As Byers said, it was clearly readable. There were Joey's small prints running toward the Academy. About twenty-five yards along the way he was stopped, apparently by a woman coming from the Academy. Joey had turned and run back toward the Cogswells'. Halfway there he was stopped again, this time by a man wearing heavy shoes with square leather heels. Once again Joey had turned back, still trying to find a way out. He seemed to have stumbled and staggered. Then all three sets of prints were involved in some sort of group struggle, and there was a place where Joey had lain flat—and bled. The stabbing, at least, had taken place there, and then there was an indication that the man had picked Joey up and carried him away. His footprints sank deeper into the wet earth. The woman was with him but no prints belonging to Joey. He must have been carried away.

"They took the boy to your cottage, George," Red Egan said.

"That was risky in the daylight," Lewis said.

"We don't know that it was daylight," Uncle George

said. "Chances are the struggle took place in the late twilight. They had to see each other for it to read the way it does. But they could have waited for darkness to carry him away."

"They just intended to let him die," Red said. "Bastards!"

"But if the boy makes it, they are done for," Lewis said. "He can tell us everything."

"We hope!" Uncle George said.

"It looks like the woman came from the Academy," Lewis said. "What is the story on the women there, Sheriff?"

Red Egan was expected to have local statistics at his fingertips, and in this case he did.

"Three cooks," he said, "three kitchen helpers, a couple of dozen younger women who double as waitresses and housemaids, three girls who handle the telephone switchboard in eight-hour shifts, four secretaries in the business office, and three faculty wives. You have met Mrs. Clark, who is one of them. A little over three dozen women if I haven't forgotten someone."

"An awful lot to check out against these footprints," Martin said.

"Could what we think are women's prints have been made by one of the boys?" Sergeant Styles asked.

"Not unless there is a boy who wears high heels," Lewis said. "Well, we had better start rounding up these dames and start trying to match these footprints."

"I'm going into town and buy myself some clothes," Uncle George said, "and then to the hospital to check on how Joey's doing."

PATTERN FOR TERROR

He drove the white Jeep to Bob's Clothing Store in the center of town. A man wearing a bathrobe, bare-footed, would have attracted considerable attention at any other time, but everyone knew about the fire and understood.

In the clothing store Uncle George bought socks, shoes, underwear, a pair of blue jeans, a canvas zip-fronted jacket, and a tweed cap.

"I'll be back for more," he told Bob. "I lost every-thing up there."

"I'm so sorry for you," Bob said, "and look for-ward to serving you."

He went next door to the hardware store and bought himself a handgun and ammunition. A local ordi-nance would have required him to wait a week to take delivery after buying a gun, but under the cir-cumstances, no one was going to make that stick.

He drove to the hospital at the outskirts of town, parked the Jeep and walked to the front entrance. Four state troopers were guarding it. He walked past them, stopped and turned.

"Aren't you checking people who walk in?" he asked.

"Hell, we don't have to check you, Mr. Crowder. We know who you are and what your concern is here."

"You are stopping others?"

"Not doctors and nurses or other hospital people we know. But everyone else."

Uncle George took his newly bought gun out of his pocket. "Nobody with weapons," Uncle George said. "The boy is still in deadly danger until he talks."

"He hasn't talked," the trooper said. "We would have been told and be looking for someone specific."

The familiar nurse was still in the little waiting room outside the emergency room where Joey was bedded down. With her was a state trooper who stood up as Uncle George walked in, grinned, and sat down again.

"Any news from inside?" Uncle George asked the nurse.

"Nothing," the nurse said. "Dr. Potter is in there now with Joey along with his parents."

Uncle George gave the trooper a grim look. "Are you letting me walk in there without searching me for a weapon?" he asked.

"Hell, why should I search you, Mr. Crowder?" the trooper asked. "If you weren't carrying a gun, I'd think you weren't doing your job."

Uncle George walked into the private room. Joey lay on his bed, his eyes closed. Dr. Potter was standing beside him, testing his pulse. Esther stood across from the doctor staring anxiously down at her small son. Hector stood by the window, holding his shotgun.

"Hail the conquering hero," Hector said in a soft mocking voice.

Esther looked up. "George! We heard about your house. How awful."

"It's totaled, I'm afraid," Uncle George said. "Joey?"

"His vital signs are doing better than we could have hoped," Dr. Potter said. "But not a spark of anything mentally."

"Is it too soon?" Uncle George asked.

"Who knows?" the doctor said. "In cases like this, all react differently. There is no schedule to go by. Sit down here by him, George, and talk to him. It just might start something ticking."

PATTERN FOR TERROR

Uncle George sat down beside Joey's bed and took the boy's small hand in his. "Joey! It's Uncle George. How are you, boy? Tell me what happened to you."

There was nothing for a moment and then Uncle George looked up at the doctor. "He is squeezing my finger!"

"Great!" the doctor said. "Keep talking. Tell him about the fire. It might shock him into some kind of response."

"Joey, my house burned down. Someone tried to burn me up while I was asleep. Then they tried to shoot me. It must have been the same people who attacked you. Can you name them, boy?"

The boy's hand fell away from Uncle George's. He was gone again.

"Maybe it was too much for him to take," Dr. Potter said. "Is there someone else he cares for like he does you—a pet animal perhaps, another person."

" 'My great Uncle George' is almost all he ever talks about," Hector said.

"There was the dead man," Uncle George said, "Alexander Francis. But Joey knows that Francis is dead. He was with him when it happened."

"That set him off playing detective like his uncle," Hector said. "That's what got him in trouble."

"He loves his records," Esther said. "Those golden oldies, maybe if he heard them—"

"The man who made those records is at the Cogswells'," Uncle George said. "Slick Evarts. Perhaps I could get him to come here and play some of them for Joey."

"It might work," the doctor said.

"I can't trust anyone," Uncle George said. "But we can make sure he doesn't harm Joey."

113

"Would he do what you ask?" Dr. Potter wanted to know.

"We can try," Uncle George said. "I'll send one of the troopers for him and have him brought here with his guitar."

"I'd like to add my five-cents worth," the doctor said. "I know you and the cops have been focusing on the Academy and the Cogswell place, but I can tell you that is not the only place to look for drug users in this town. The three other doctors and I, who practice here in Lakeview, know that there are many drug users here in town. Lots of patients who come to any one of us with a problem have the symptoms of drug use. The whole town is involved. We have been urging the state police to put a stop to it."

"That is what's so dangerous," Uncle George said. "As long as we don't jump someone and put them in jail, they know Joey hasn't talked. They know that sooner or later he may recover enough to name them. They will do anything they have to do to stop him before that happens."

"If this man Evarts will sing for Joey, it just might bring him around," the doctor said.

"Why not send out the word that Joey has come to and is talking," Hector said. "It would be too late for them then."

"But if we haven't made an arrest, or hold the wrong people, they'll know he is still dangerous to them," Uncle George said.

"Well, get your singer here and let's see what happens," Dr. Potter said.

It took almost an hour for a trooper to locate Slick

Evarts and bring him back to the hospital, carrying his guitar as Uncle George had requested. At the front door Uncle George turned to the trooper.

"Weapons search," he said.

"Already done," the trooper said.

"In my presence," Uncle George said.

Evarts held out his arms, holding his guitar in his right hand, and the trooper slapped over his clothes.

"Clean," he said.

"The guitar," Uncle George said.

The trooper took the instrument and shook it. "Clean," he said.

Evarts lowered his arms, grinning. "Don't you want to look between my teeth?" he asked.

"I can't make you do what I'm asking," Uncle George said. "But if the boy hears one of your golden oldies being played by you, it just might stir up some of his memory processes."

"He liked my music, I'd like to help him," Evarts said.

Uncle George led the way into the room. Dr. Potter and Esther and Hector were still there. Uncle George led Evarts over to the bed.

"Joey! I've brought Slick Evarts to see you. He'd like to sing for you."

The boy lay perfectly still, his eyes closed.

"Is there one he likes—besides 'Robinson Crusoe'?" Evarts asked.

"One called 'Row,'" Uncle George said.

Evarts nodded, sat down beside the bed, and began to strum rhythmic chords on the guitar and sing softly.

Hugh Pentecost

"Young Johnny Jones he had a cute little boat,
And all the girlies he would take for a float.
He had girlies on the shore,
Sweet little peaches by the score.
But Johnny was a wisenheimer you know,
His steady girl was Flo.
He would ask her to his boat,
She would happily float,
And they would go, row, row.
And they would row, row, row.
Way up the river they would go, go, go.
A hug he'd give her, then kiss her now and then,
She would tell him when,
They'd fool around and fool around,
And then they'd kiss again.
And then they'd row, row, row,
Way up the river they would go, go, go."

Evarts stopped singing but kept the chords going on his guitar. "I'm sorry, Joey, but I've forgotten the last couple of lines of that lyric."

Joey opened his eyes. They were very bright. His lips moved, and the sound of the song came from them.

"He would drop both his oars,
Take a few more encores,
And then he'd row, row, row."

"Exactly right, Joey," Evarts said. "How could I have forgotten?" Behind him Dr. Potter was holding up both hands, fists clenched in a gesture of victory.

"He has remembered something from long before what has happened to him," Potter said. "The more recent things may be just around the corner."

"Is there anything more I can do to help?" Evarts asked.

"Tell me about the drug dealings at the Cogswells'."

Evarts shrugged. "I've already told you that no one there, including the girls, could afford the kind of load Alex Francis was carrying in his gut. But crack and marijuana? The tradesmen who deliver are anyone who strolls in. The town is loaded with them."

"Name a couple," Uncle George said.

"I'm not a user," Evarts said. "I don't buy so I haven't paid any direct attention. I don't have names for the tradespeople. I don't deal with them."

"So I'm ordering you to stay here," Uncle George said. "I can't have you wandering around out there telling people the boy is close to remembering. That could place him in the gravest danger."

"If I promised you not to tell anyone?"

"I can't risk it," Uncle George said.

"If I promise not to tell anyone that the boy is recovering?"

"Anyone who knows you have been here will be asking," Uncle George said. "Even if you don't talk, your face might reveal the answer."

"Do you have the authority to keep me here?" Evarts asked, his face hardening.

"I've been deputized by the state police, the FBI, and the local sheriff," Uncle George said. "I have the authority and I will instruct the troopers to see to it that you obey."

Evarts shrugged. "So I'll sing some more for the boy and see if we can wake him up a little further."

Evarts began to strum some fast rhythms on his guitar and sing.

> "Somebody stole my gal,
> Somebody stole my pal,
> Somebody came and took her away,
> She didn't even
> Say she was leavin'."

He nodded to Joey and stopped singing. The boy took over in his frail little voice.

> "The kisses I love so,
> He's getting now, I know.
> Oh gee, I wish that she
> Could only see me,
> Her brokenhearted lonesome pal.
> Somebody stole my gal."

"Perfect," Evarts said.

Joey closed his eyes again. Uncle George made a saluting gesture to Evarts and walked out of the room. He gave instructions to the trooper in the waiting room and the ones at the front door that Evarts was not to be allowed to leave. And no one unless accompanied by him, Captain Lewis, Sergeant Styles, or Red Egan was to be admitted. Not anyone!

And then he walked out to the parking lot. This had been his town all his life, but it was no longer the place he remembered and loved. This was a place of drugs, violence, and terror. Anyone he passed on the street could be the person who had tried to kill Joey, burned his cottage, and attempted to shoot him to death. Old friends could be his mortal enemies. It was sickening, he thought.

He walked slowly around the corner of the building to where he had left his Jeep. Someone was standing by it, someone he had not expected to see. It was Leona Boyd, the heartbroken girl who had been Alex Francis's lover.

"I was so sorry to hear about your fire," she said, as he joined her.

"Thanks."

"Has the boy come to?"

Uncle George shook his head.

"Have you found any lead to the people who left those footprints on the lake shore?"

He shook his head again. Then he cursed himself silently. He should have known better than to answer either of those questions in any fashion. If she passed it along, the would-be killers would know there was still time in which to silence Joey—permanently.

"I wanted to talk to you," Leona said, "because I have had to admit to myself that you were right earlier. My Alex couldn't have swallowed the heroin by accident. He must have known what he was doing."

"Which means?"

"That he was being blackmailed or terrorized by someone. Alex would never have become involved in such an operation voluntarily. It would have been completely out of character."

"Blackmailed about what?" Uncle George asked.

"I can't imagine. He was so clean, so open and aboveboard."

"Terrorized by what?"

"Perhaps by someone threatening to harm me," the girl said. "Telling him I would be hurt if he didn't follow orders."

"And he wouldn't tell you?"

"So I would live in panic every day of my life? Alex loved me, he cherished me."

"And you have no idea who might have been making these threats or why?"

"I've done nothing but try to think it out since Alex died," the girl said. "Obviously these Friday trips were the key to it all. As you know, I've had some time for conversation with Joshua Willis, the headmaster here at the Academy. His story is the same one I heard from Alex when it all began. Willis needed a first-rate English teacher. He called his friend David Ash at Columbia and asked if he could recommend someone. Ash recommended Alex, highly. But there was a hitch. If Willis liked him, Alex would have to complete the term of his Friday night class at Columbia. It really wasn't any problem. The academic day at the Academy ended at three in the afternoon. Alex would have plenty of time to get to New York for his Friday night class and be back for his Saturday morning duties. Willis was impressed with Alex and hired him. Ash set it all up and Ash has to be the one who put the heat on Alex and turned him into a drug handler. He has to have been the one who frightened Alex into complying. Can't we confront him and turn a few screws?"

Uncle George glanced at his wristwatch, the one possession left from the fire. He'd been wearing it.

"The school day will be over there."

"Night classes," the girl said. "That is what Alex had. A night class. You might be able to make Ash talk."

It would take a couple of hours to make the round trip to New York. A half hour with David Ash might clear away some of the fog. There were enough troopers and local lawmen to surround Joey with protection. Perhaps, as Leona suggested, he could put enough heat on David Ash to get some facts out of him.

"Let's go," he said.

Leona got into the passenger seat and Uncle George drove around to the front door guarded by the squad of troopers. He spoke to the sergeant in charge.

"If you see Sheriff Egan, tell him I've gone into New York to follow up on a lead. I should be back in three or four hours. Understand, no one is to go in to see that boy. Not someone you know well, not your best friend, not the President of the United States."

The trooper grinned. "Should Mr. Bush be interested?"

"He should. We are fighting drugs, our worst enemy. The boy may eventually help win the war."

The trip to New York was uneventful. The heaviest traffic was coming out of the city, suburbanites returning home from work. It occurred to Uncle George that it was just about this time Saturday that a man and woman chased Joey along the lake shore, beat, stabbed, and left him for dead—and later set fire to his house and taken a shot at him. A fierce surge of anger swept over him. He reached down to his side pocket and felt the gun he had recently bought. If he had to use it to settle a score with David Ash, he just might—just might.

In the city they drove down crowded Broadway to the Columbia campus and stopped outside the building that housed the Extension office.

"I suggest you talk to him alone," Leona said. "I don't think he ever thought of me as one of Alex Francis's primary assets. He might try to put on some kind of act if he had to talk about personal matters to a woman. Man-to-man might get better results."

"Worth a try," Uncle George said.

He went in. There was no sign of David Ash in the office. A secretary asked him what she could do for him.

"Mr. Ash," he said.

"He's not here," the girl said. "He goes home every night at this time to rest for evening classes and business."

"Where is his home?"

"Why should I tell you?" the girl asked.

"I am a deputy state trooper. This is police business."

The girl hesitated a moment. "Riverside Drive and One hundred fifteenth Street," she said. "Four hundred thirty-one Riverside. Apartment seven C."

One hundred fifteenth Street is a steep hill from Broadway down to the Drive, facing the Hudson River. Uncle George left Leona in the Jeep and walked into 431. Elevators were at the rear of the entrance, self-service. He was whisked up to seven, walked along the corridor to apartment C, and rang the doorbell.

The door was opened instantly by someone standing just inside. It was David Ash.

"So what is it now?" Ash asked.

"I have some suspicions about you," Uncle George said. "If they hold up, I'll be bringing charges against you."

"Charges?" Ash laughed. "I know quite a lot about you from talking to Joshua Willis," he said. "You used to be the prosecuting attorney up there in Lakeview—until you sent an innocent man to the gas chamber. Charges?"

"I suspect you of turning Alexander Francis into a distributor of illegal substances," Uncle George said. "When he died, I think you went up to Lakeview to make sure the trail didn't lead to you. In some fashion, God help me I don't know how, my ten-year-old nephew got on that trail. You and a lady friend of yours chased him down, beat him, stabbed him, and left him for dead on the doorstep of my cottage."

"Oh, boy!" Ash said.

"Later you set fire to that cottage when you knew I was resting there, then took a shot at me when I escaped the fire."

"You believe all that?" Ash asked.

"The best answer I can come to," Uncle George said.

"Let's settle it," Ash said. "This all happened Saturday?"

"Yes."

"I can produce more than a dozen witnesses who can swear there was no way I could have been in Lakeview at any time Saturday. Not any time! I can't have been involved with any of the things you say happened to the boy and you."

"So produce the witnesses," Uncle George said.

"Not for you, but for the police," Ash said. "I don't

123

trust what you might do with any kind of evidence I give to you. Your history suggests you can make any kind of evidence work your way. There is a police station north on Broadway. Go up there, get them to send a cop down here, and I'll produce my alibi. He can check it out."

"You wait here—stay here," Uncle George said. "If you don't, I might just decide to settle this whole thing on a personal basis."

"I'm sure a man who can make your kind of mistakes could do just that," Ash said. "I'll be here when the cops come."

It wasn't a bad idea, Uncle George thought. Witnesses answering questions from him would have had it made clear to them by Ash that George was the enemy. A police inquiry would be harder to duck.

He left Ash, took the elevator down to the lobby, and walked out onto the street. Leona Boyd wasn't sitting in the Jeep where he had left her. He looked up and down the block. No sign of her. There were no shops where she might be windowshopping. Then he remembered that she had an apartment somewhere in this area. She may have thought she had time enough to get something she needed. Well, he could go up to the police station, present his case against Ash, and then come back for her.

He got into the Jeep, put his key in the ignition, and turned it to start the motor.

There was a violent explosion. The whole front of the Jeep blew skyward—engine and windshield. Uncle George was hurled out of the driver's seat onto the stone pavement fronting Ash's apartment building. It was so violent he suddenly hurt from head to foot.

He reached out blindly. Glass and bits of hot metal were raining down around him. He found himself gripping something that felt like an iron fence rail. He tried to pull himself up by it. Instead, he fell down a short flight of iron steps and lay outside what must be a cellar door. He reached up and tried the doorknob that was above his head. The door wasn't locked and it pushed open easily. He opened it with his feet and fell again into an area of total darkness. He reached down to feel for his gun. He had fallen hard on it up at the street level. It was there, but it felt broken.

This was a second attempt on his life, and he knew it. If anyone had seen him fall from the street level, they would be coming down here after him. He was too badly hurt to defend himself without a gun. He would be as good as dead at the hands of these monsters.

7.

Uncle George lay in the darkness at the bottom of the steps, hurting from head to toe. He tried moving his legs. It was agony, but they moved. He was able to draw them up, bent at the knees. He rolled over, face down, and then managed to kneel. His back was in agony, but eventually he was able to stand. He had to stop thinking about his physical difficulties and concentrate on his battle with a murderer. Whatever he might think about David Ash's connection with the Lakeview violences, he couldn't have been personally involved with blowing up the Jeep. When he had arrived at 431 Riverside, he had left Leona Boyd in the Jeep and gone up to apartment seven. Ash had been right at the apartment door. No way he could have planted the bomb while Uncle George was going up the stairs, or could he have planted it while Uncle George was headed down to the Jeep to leave. Of course someone working for

Ash, some ally in the chain of crimes, could have managed it. But with Leona sitting there waiting for him? It was then that a new light focused on the situation. A woman had been involved in the attack on Joey. A woman with high heels who had left her footprints on the lakeshore. Like a damn fool he hadn't looked at Leona's shoes, but she had been in Lakeview at that time. He had brought her there himself. She hadn't been in his car when it blew up. Did she know it was coming? Had she planted the bomb herself while he went upstairs to confront Ash? Was she an enemy and not an ally? He had himself driven her to Lakeview Saturday. She had been there, somewhere, when Joey was attacked, when the cottage was burned, when someone had fired a shot at him. And she had been in the Jeep or somewhere close by when the bomb blew up. She was either in the garbage that had rained down around the Jeep, or she had planted the bomb and was waiting in safety to see what had happened to Uncle George, her intended victim.

He could hear sounds from the street—excited voices shouting back and forth to one another. Had anyone but Leona seen him get into the Jeep and turn the key which was meant to bring about the end of everything for him? If someone else had seen him, they might have seen her and what she'd been up to. It wouldn't have caused any excitement to see a woman examining the motor of her car—but what about a few minutes later when it blew sky-high?

There must be some other way out of this basement than the way he had come, Uncle George thought. His enemies were undoubtedly watching the street where the Jeep had exploded, hoping the police would come up with pieces of him in the wreckage. If he left that way, he would just be making a target of himself once more. He couldn't hope, he thought, for his good luck to last forever. Joey was alive, the fire at his house hadn't consumed him, the bullet that had nicked his shoulder had been meant for his brain, and the bomb up on the street had been meant for his total destruction. They must be telling themselves that they just couldn't miss another time.

He began to feel his way along the black wall, hoping to come on a door that would lead him somewhere. Nothing at first. And then he came to an irregularity. It was bigger than a house door and he guessed an elevator. He felt around for a signal button and found it. His hand was unsteady as he pressed the lower button. Almost instantly he heard something like machinery in action. Then there was light from a transom over the door as a freight elevator moved into place and the door opened toward him, almost knocking him off his unsteady legs. He shuffled into the car and pressed the very top button on the switchboard. The car started up fairly briskly. It wouldn't stop until they reached the top of the shaft. Tenants in the building wouldn't be likely to use the freight elevator, especially during all the excitement down on the street.

The car kept going up, finally stopping. The door opened and Uncle George stepped out onto the roof of the building. He had to squint against the late afternoon sun that shone brightly on the Hudson River, down and to the west of him.

Luck worked his way for the first time, Uncle George thought. The roof of 431 was at least a story higher than the buildings around him. No one could be looking out windows nearby and see him. He could move freely to try to decide what would come next.

He moved to the other side of the roof, almost forgetting how badly it still hurt for him to move at all. There he found a fire escape that led down between 431 and the building next to it. He managed to climb onto it and go down one story to the roof of the next building. From there he could see the tops of traffic moving along busy Broadway. If only he could get to a pay phone where he could call Red Egan in Lakeview for help!

There appeared to be no elevator on this second roof, only a toolshed painted red. Behind that was a door leading into the house. It was apparently also an apartment building.

He decided to stay with the stairway rather than signal for the inside elevator. By some miracle, or changing luck, he didn't encounter anyone all the way down to street level, and there he found real good fortune. Through the glass top of the lobby door he could see a pay phone booth on the street corner, standing empty. He moved quickly through the door and to the booth where he put in a collect call to Red Egan. And then, oh joy, Red's voice.

"George! Oh, God, where are you, man? We've been going crazy here. The New York police have called us about the bombing. They don't know and we had no way—Oh, man, are you all right?"

129

"Hearing your voice is enough to make me feel all right," Uncle George said. "I sound like a long lost girlfriend, don't I? I got extra lucky, Red. Pretty badly tossed around, but not critically hurt. How is Joey?"

"No real change," Red said. "He still responds to his musical friend, but Doc Potter can't bring back anything about what happened to him."

"He must be very carefully guarded, Red. These people are wild. They might even bomb the hospital room where Joey is."

"There are plenty of troopers around," Red said.

"It could involve someone who has ready access to the hospital," Uncle George warned.

"You got someone in mind?"

"Not yet," Uncle George said. "But if that Leona Boyd shows up anywhere, don't let her out of your sight. She's my prime suspect for the bombing down here."

"What next?" Red asked.

"I want to get home," Uncle George said. "I have no way of protecting myself or fighting back in a city of millions. I would go to the police here, but they might hold me because of the bombing. Time might be a threat to Joey's life."

"Where are you calling from?" Red asked.

"A pay phone at the corner of One hundred sixteenth Street and Broadway."

"Stay where you are. I've got friends in New York, George. I'll have the police get you out and bring you home. Don't move from where you are. Ten—fifteen minutes should do it."

Uncle George stood in the booth, the receiver held

to his ear, his left forefinger on the receiver hook. He was talking to himself. Several people came toward the booth, looked disappointed, and walked away. But an old woman with a shopping bag overloaded with groceries stood outside, obviously talking to Uncle George, who could not hear her. After a moment she pounded on the door and beckoned to him to come out. He shook his head, indicated the receiver, and turned his back on her. She apparently decided to camp out on him. She sat down on a radiator across from the booth, and waited, talking angrily to herself or anyone else who might hear her. About fifteen minutes later, the lady now in a frenzy, two men in civilian clothes appeared and headed straight for the booth. The first man took hold of the door handle and wrenched it open.

"Crowder?" he asked.

Uncle George nodded.

"Sergeant Patterson, NYPD," the man said. He held out his hand, palm up, revealing his police badge. "This is Officer Culp," he said. "Your man in Lakeview reached us and we are ordered to get you out of here."

"You may just be making targets of yourselves," Uncle George said.

"You walk right behind me," Patterson said. "Culp will walk behind you. We'll be ready." He pulled his gun out of its holster and Culp did the same.

But the old woman was not to be denied. "He's a criminal. I knew it!" she almost screamed. "Is he the one who blew up that car down on the Drive?"

"Don't interfere, lady," Patterson said.

The woman turned and shouted to the people who

were watching. "They have arrested the mad bomber!" People began to crowd toward the booth.

"Attracting attention to us isn't going to do any good," Uncle George said.

"If they stay with us it will be pretty hard for anyone to get to you," Patterson said.

"Unless one of them is after me," Uncle George said.

"My car is just a few steps away at the corner," Patterson said. "Let's go."

He moved with Uncle George right behind him, and Culp in tandem. They were surrounded by curious watchers. The old woman was right beside Uncle George.

"I knew you were faking that phone call. Why did you kill the man in the car?"

They reached the corner and Patterson walked around to the driver's side, while Culp opened the passenger door for Uncle George, who got in but couldn't close the door because the old woman had stepped off the curb, and was standing so the door couldn't be shut.

"I hope they burn you!" she shouted.

"If you don't want to be dragged behind us, you better move back, madam," Culp said. He gave the woman a shove and she sat down hard on the curb, her groceries spilling into her lap. Patterson started the car and Culp got in the rear door on the move.

They circled and moved up Broadway. Uncle George drew a deep breath.

"Glad to leave here, but there are two people in this area I don't like leaving," he said.

Patterson gave him a quick, questioning glance.

PATTERN FOR TERROR

"David Ash, the man I came to see and suspect of crimes in my town, and the lady who came with me who may very well have set the bomb in my Jeep."

"Ash was in the police station when I left there," Patterson said. "No, we didn't arrest him. He came there on his own. He told us you had been with him just before the bombing, had charged him with crimes in Lakeview. He says he has a list of people who can provide him with an alibi that would blow your suspicions. But there hasn't been time to find the people and question them. We got the call from your sheriff and I was ordered to get to you and cover you."

"They'll check out," Uncle George said. "Either he is innocent and really does have an alibi, or his witnesses are part of his organization and are prepared in advance to lie for him about crimes he did commit."

"Ash is well known in this part of town, Columbia being in our precinct. One person may say he was in a class, but there would be forty or fifty others who could say he was or wasn't. The girl?"

"I think she set me up for that bomb, or placed it herself. I'd love to get a pair of her shoes. There are tracks up in the country that could nail her to the cross if she's guilty."

"She, too, has talked to us," Patterson said. "She was on the scene almost before the police got there, screaming for help to find you. She had seen you blown out of the Jeep."

"Why didn't she follow me down into the basement?"

"Perhaps because she didn't see you," Patterson said. "She claims she was waiting in the Jeep when

133

you went upstairs in 431 to talk with Ash. She expected you to be quite a while. She saw that from the corner of One hundred sixteenth Street, just north, there was a magnificent view of the river and the bridge. She walked up there, looking back all the time in case you returned. She'd been standing a block away for a few minutes when she saw you come out of the building and get in the Jeep. She started down the block to join you and the bomb went off. She saw you hurled out, turned away in shock, and then ran down the street, sure she'd find you in pieces."

"It won't hold," Uncle George said. "The Jeep was parked headed north. If she'd been standing just a block away, I'd have seen her. I was looking for her. She was wearing a bright yellow sports shirt and a blue jean skirt. No missing her. She wasn't there."

"The precinct captain had no reason to doubt her," Patterson said. "At that time we also expected to find you in pieces."

"So you let her go?"

Patterson nodded. "No reason not to."

"She will have had plenty of time to get safely hidden," Uncle George said.

"If she doesn't try to go anyplace," Patterson said. "Enough of us saw her to make her easy to identify."

"She has an apartment somewhere in the area. You might be able to get a pair of shoes from it. I don't know exactly where it is, but she may be in the phone book—if her name is really Leona Boyd."

"She gave the captain an address," Patterson said.

They drove on up through Van Cortlandt Park and onto the highway that would take them to Lakeview.

PATTERN FOR TERROR

"I don't know why you will be safer up here," Patterson said. "Your young nephew was nearly murdered in Lakeview, your house was burned down, a shot that nicked your shoulder was only inches away from being fatal."

"There will be faces of people I know and trust. That will make me feel better whether it makes me safer or not."

There would be Red Egan, Lieutenant Lewis, Sergeant Styles, Esther, and even Hector Trimble. Even Hector wouldn't be able to take the situation lightly. The countryside got more and more familiar. Uncle George had driven this road a thousand times in his life. Eventually they were driving up Lakeview's main street toward the hospital. Uncle George had insisted on going there before they went to the sheriff's office. He had to know about Joey.

A group of troopers guarded the entrance. They were the same ones Uncle George had left there it seemed nearly three years ago. They quickly surrounded Patterson's car.

"After what we heard, it's good to see you, Mr. Crowder." That was the trooper he'd left instructions with about guarding Joey.

"Anything new about the boy?" Uncle George asked.

"I've heard nothing," the trooper said.

Patterson and Culp went in the emergency room with Uncle George. The same nurse and trooper were in the waiting room. Both of them expressed pleasure at seeing him safe. The news had been pretty shocking until Red Egan let them know that his friend had made it out alive.

In the inner room Joey still lay on his bed, with

Slick Evarts sitting by him. Esther came running and threw her arms around her brother.

"Oh, George, thank God!" she whispered.

Hector stood by the door, fondling his shotgun. Dr. Potter was over by the window, and made a little gesture of greeting. Uncle George went over to the bed and took Joey's hand. The small boy opened his eyes and they brightened. His fingers tightened on Uncle George's hand.

"Joey boy."

Joey smiled.

"In a few years, if this boy learns to sing as well as he can remember lyrics," Evarts said, "you'll have a nightclub star on your hands."

Uncle George glanced at Dr. Potter. The doctor shook his head. "That's all," he said. "I haven't been able to bring out the memory of what happened earlier."

"His physical condition?"

"A small miracle. It looks as if he is pretty much out of danger."

"I think we should get him moved from here if we can," Uncle George said. "These bastards may try to blow this place up."

"How do we get him out of here without their knowing?" Red Egan asked. "After what has happened here, and in New York, half the town is watching for what happens next. It is still possible the killers are my best friends, hooked on drugs."

"I think there is a way to move him," Dr. Potter said, "to my house. I have my private office there, you know. The hospital sends me supplies from time to time. We can put Joey in a linen basket and move him over there. I have a nurse-secretary on duty who can watch over him, and I can take care of him there."

"He goes nowhere without me," Esther said, her voice unsteady.

"Everyone knows you, Mrs. Trimble," Potter said, "but dressed as a nurse, I think you could be driven right past your closest friend. She wouldn't be expecting you to be dressed that way."

"I go too," Hector said, massaging his shotgun.

"I suggest you stay right here and let yourself be seen," Dr. Potter said. "People will think you are still protecting the boy."

"Let's move it," Uncle George said. He bent over the child's bed. "We're taking you to Doc Potter's, Joey. You heard?"

The boy nodded.

Dr. Potter was on the phone. A few minutes later a staff member came in with a large laundry cart. A nurse appeared with a uniform for Esther. Joey was lifted from his bed by Dr. Potter and placed in the laundry basket. He prepared to cover the boy with a sheet.

"Don't be frightened, Joey," he said. "We don't want anyone to know that we are moving you."

The child opened his eyes, looking for Uncle George. Uncle George reached out and took Joey's hand. "I won't ever be far away, Joey."

The boy closed his eyes and heaved a deep sigh of relief. He was covered with a sheet and the basket was wheeled out to a truck waiting in the parking lot outside the emergency room. People watched, but they weren't interested in hospital laundry. A moment later the truck drove away with Esther, a nurse now, riding beside the driver. There was every reason to believe their ruse had worked perfectly.

Dr. Potter reached in his pocket and pulled out a ring of keys. He detached one and held it out to Uncle George.

"A key to the kitchen door, George," he said. "Use it to come and go. But be careful. You certainly will be watched."

"What's the next move?" Patterson asked. "If you don't need me, I should be heading back to my post in New York."

"I don't like to see any help backing away," Uncle George said, "but I suppose everyone knows you are a New York cop."

What *was* the next move? Find Leona Boyd and identify the man who had been her partner in the beating of Joey. He could be anyone here in town.

"One person Leona had contact with here was Joshua Willis," Red Egan said. "He and Ash set up Francis on his double teaching routine, and his Friday night trips. Could he—?"

"One of the most respected people here in Lakeview," Dr. Potter said. "If you are suggesting he might have anything to do with Francis carrying illegal substances, you're off your rocker, Red. You all know Willis. He owns a big piece of this hospital. He came here to inquire about the boy, but the troopers wouldn't let him in. Crowder had said not even the President of the United States. Willis laughed, but I think he was a little upset. He is more important to Lakeview than the President. He supports all the major charities, and he has rescued dozens of homeless and underprivileged boys. In fact we don't have many of them, thanks to him. Charge him with any sort of crime, and you will have this whole community on your backs."

"But he might be able to tell us something about Leona Boyd," Uncle George said. "He spent some time with her."

"Ask him," Dr. Potter said. "He might turn out to be the strongest ally you could have in town."

That was certainly a sensible suggestion, Uncle George thought. "I'll go over to the Academy," he said. "Keep Hector here in view. It will persuade anybody who is watching that he's here to protect Joey. Thanks for your help and your advice, Doc." He shook his head. "I've got to borrow a car. After today, I don't have very much left that I owned this morning."

"I'll drive you to the Academy on my way back to the city," Patterson said.

He and Culp and Uncle George went down to the city police car in the parking lot.

"This man Willis sounds almost too good to be true," Patterson said as they headed across town toward the big school.

"The town feels very lucky to have him," Uncle George said. "There has never been any difficult problem where he hasn't put his shoulder to the wheel."

"I've learned never to be sure of the people who look so good," Patterson said.

The two New York cops left Uncle George outside the Academy office building. Uncle George knew the school grounds well. When he had first come back to Lakeview after he had gone away following his court

139

disaster, he had a job here as a groundskeeper. Willis had been his boss though they'd had no personal contact. He knew that Willis had suggested hiring him. It was one of his gestures of help toward someone in trouble. Uncle George had always felt he owed him.

Willis was in his office, and his secretary announced the visitor. Uncle George was ushered in. Willis was seated at his big mahogany desk.

"Glad you dropped by," Willis said. "I was kept from seeing your nephew at your orders, I understand. 'Not even the President!' "

"A careless word about his condition might have placed him in greater danger than he already is in," Uncle George said. "He is doing well, but he hasn't remembered what happened to him."

"I understand one of the musicians from the Cogswells' is there with him," Willis said.

"Where did you hear that?"

"From Dolly and Molly. He apparently rates ahead of the President and me."

"Part of the doctor's attempt to restore his memory," Uncle George said. "Joey had collected some of Slick Evarts's records, and he loved them. We thought if Slick would sing for him, it might stir what's stuck in his head."

"And did it?"

"He remembered lyrics, actually sang a little with Slick. But it didn't loosen anything else."

"Anything to do with those words the boy spoke when the kidnapper put him on the phone with you? 'Friday on Saturday'?"

"Where did Robinson Crusoe go With Friday on

Saturday Night? Joey and I had a joke about where that would be if they were in Lakeview. He thought the Cogswells'. 'Where there are wild men, there must be wild women.' "

Willis chuckled. "Quite a boy," he said. "But Evarts is still there. I asked when I stopped to see the boy."

"We don't want him spreading the word that the boy hasn't remembered what happened to him. That would leave him still a target."

"But you are now willing to tell me?"

"It has been pointed out to me that you are more important in this town than the President," Uncle George said. "That is why you might be able to help me more than anyone else."

"Tell me where to start," Willis said.

"With Leona Boyd," Uncle George said.

Willis's shaggy eyebrows rose. "Alex Francis's girl?"

"Yes. I have reason to believe she may have been connected with the bombing of my Jeep in New York."

"Reason to believe?"

"Her story doesn't match the facts. She should have been in the Jeep with me when it happened. She luckily or on purpose was safely away when it happened."

"But how can I help with her?" Willis asked. "I never laid eyes on her until you brought her up here from the city Saturday and left her to mingle among us."

"You knew Francis had a girl?"

"Yes, I knew. It's part of the checklist when we hire a new teacher. I can't have love affairs being

141

carried on in front of four hundred impressionable boys."

"Leona never came to see Francis here?"

"If she did, it was managed secretly. I have a small army of what you might call intelligence operators who report anything irregular that may happen on my campus."

"She was clinging pretty tight to you the last time I saw you together," Uncle George said.

"Trying to sell me on a hopeless dream," Willis said. "She was still trying to say Francis had accidentally swallowed the drug that killed him. She shifted to another story when they found the second pouch in his gut. He had been blackmailed or terrorized into being a drug carrier."

"She made the same suggestion to me," Uncle George said.

"I couldn't buy it," Willis said. "There is too much money involved to need terror as a weapon."

"Who do you suppose she was trying to save his reputation for?" Uncle George said. "He wasn't ever going to apply for a teaching job or any other kind of job again. He didn't have any family. Parents, brothers and sisters."

"My records show no one," Willis said. "We have a who-to-notify-in-case-of-sickness-or-accident file on all employees. The only name in his file was the president of his bank in New York—Irving Trust. We let him know yesterday. There was nothing he could do. He didn't know if Francis had a will, but he did have a lawyer. That lawyer is out of town somewhere on a business trip. Can't be reached. He is not expected back for a few days."

PATTERN FOR TERROR

"As you know, we have evidence that a woman was involved in the beating and stabbing of Joey Trimble," Uncle George said. "If it wasn't Leona, it was someone who came from the direction of your campus. Any ideas?"

"None," Willis said. "The local cops have been questioning all the women we employ—nearly three dozen of them. I've had some complaints but of course the police have every right to do their duty."

"What about drugs at the Academy?" Uncle George asked.

Will shook his head. "A nightmare!" he said. "I know what everyone else knows about the whole town and drugs. But I have hundreds of boys to protect. We do constant spot checks."

"And the result?"

"One or two every time we check," Willis said. "They know that drugs come from killer mobs like the Mafia and God knows who else. You know, Crowder, things are different than they were in the days of Prohibition. The bootleggers were arrested and prosecuted. The people who drank went untouched. They have turned it around with drugs. The user gets arrested. The taker like that All-American defensive back on the New York Giants—Lawrence Taylor? He gets suspended and wonders, not whether he will get back to football, but what will happen to the rest of his life. The people who sold drugs to him and kept his habit alive, go scot-free. It is too dangerous to go after them, we don't have adequate police who are properly trained. Our big-shot politicians don't have the courage to really fight this curse.

Suspend, fire, and punish the users. Let the people who are getting rich from it go untouched."

"Back to Leona Boyd, if you don't mind," Uncle George said. "Does it seem possible to you that she was a fake from the start? That she knew all along what her man was doing, might even have shared in it with him? She wanted to clear him so he would drop out of the picture and nothing would lead to her."

"She must not have thought it had worked if she tried to blow you up in your Jeep," Willis said.

"I need solid evidence that I haven't got yet," Uncle George said. "From the very start I've been playing a guessing game."

"The local cops have taken enough shoes from my workers' closets to set up a shoe store," Willis said. "You need a pair of the Boyd woman's shoes, surely the New York police can get a warrant to search her apartment."

"More important would be to find her again and keep her in custody. She went to them and told them her bogus story after the bombing and they let her go!" Uncle George said.

"That gave her time to collect her money and run," Willis said. "If she can get her hands on Francis's money or if they had a joint account, she may be a very rich woman. But if she has a claim to Francis's money she'll have to go through her bank and his lawyer. That is where your New York cops can pick her up. I can give them the banker's name and his branch of Irving Trust. He can give them the lawyer."

"Let's move on it," Uncle George said. "I'll phone

the information to Sergeant Patterson. He should be getting back to his headquarters pretty soon."

Willis went to a filing cabinet behind his desk and took out a folder after fingering through several.

"The banker is George McCloud." Willis looked surprised. "I have the lawyer's name here, too. Bernard Vulosovich. As a matter of fact, I recommended him to Francis."

"You know him then?"

"Not really. He handled a damage suit that was brought against us by one of our boys' parents. He lost the suit, but I was impressed with him. I asked him if he would handle some odds and ends that come up for us in the city. He said he would and he has."

"Then you can get information from him about any will Francis may have left."

"I can try."

Willis sat down at his desk again and dialed a number on his phone. It seemed to take a while after it must have started ringing. "Answering service," he said. Then he leaned forward. "This is Joshua Willis at the Lakeview Academy in Lakeview. I need to reach Mr. Vulosovich. It is an emergency." He listened and hung up. "He's gone on a holiday, and won't be back until next week. They will let him know I called." Willis dialed the number again, and waited. "This is Joshua Willis again. I know Mr. Vulosovich isn't there, but can I speak to his secretary or anyone else in charge of the office?" He waited again, and then hung up the phone. "The whole office staff has chosen to vacation along with the boss. We will have to wait."

"And Leona Boyd can be at the other end of the world with her money," Uncle George said.

"It can be a luxury trip if what you think is true," Willis said.

"I wonder if she got to Vulosovich before he took off," Uncle George said.

"Why were you dangerous to her? Why the bomb?" Willis asked.

"Joey could have talked."

"But he hasn't, and almost everyone in town knows it."

"But I am the person who could break that silence," Uncle George said. "Joey would do anything I asked him if he were able."

"Well, he is there in the hospital," Willis said. "Shouldn't you be spending all your time with him, trying to help him remember?"

It was a sensible suggestion. Uncle George moved toward the door. "Thanks for all your help," he said.

"None of it is going to do you much good," Willis said.

"When Vulosovich gets back on the job—perhaps," Uncle George said.

"That may be too late. These bastards have turned our village into a murder mall. Are you armed?" Willis asked.

"With a broken gun, I think," Uncle George replied.

"Let me help you out." Willis turned to a closet and opened the door. Uncle George saw a rack with a dozen or more handguns on it. Willis took out one of them and checked the loading chamber. "This should place you at least at even," he said, handing Uncle George the gun.

"Thanks, and thanks again."

Uncle George hesitated at the door. "Do you have a car I could borrow? I have no way of getting around since the bombing."

Willis reached in his pocket and took out a key ring. He took off two keys and handed them to Uncle George. "There is a Mazda convertible in the garage, if you don't mind the fresh air."

"Thanks, and thanks, and thanks," Uncle George said and left.

Dr. Potter's house was at the north end of the village, down a narrow country lane. The road looked well traveled by the Doc's patients, but there was no car in sight when Uncle George drove up to the back door. He left the car and let himself in with the key Potter had given him.

Dr. Potter's kitchen was as neat and orderly as Uncle George would have expected. He walked across it and pushed open the swinging door that led into the front of the house. It was a combination living room and dining room, with bookcased walls loaded with hundreds of books. That was how Potter must spend his free time—reading.

A side door opened and Esther's voice called out his name. "George!" She looked unfamiliar in her nurse's uniform.

"I hoped you would come, George."

"Soon as I could. I was trying to run down something about the Boyd woman from Joshua Willis."

"Does he know where she is?"

"No, but he gave me a lead to someone who may. How is Joey?"

"Very restless, George," Esther said. "He seems to

want his singer man, and I thought I heard him say the word 'uncle.' He's right in here."

Joey looked very small, bedded down in Dr. Potter's big four-poster bed. Uncle George sat down on the edge of the bed and took the boy's hand.

"Joey."

The boy's eyes opened, looked very bright, and his lips moved in a smile. "Uncle George," he whispered.

That was the first time he had spoken anything that was a sign of recognition.

"Well, boy, high time you said hello," Uncle George said. "Can you talk now? Can you tell me things I need to know?"

The boy hesitated. "I'll try," he said.

Uncle George looked at Esther and grinned. Things might be about to happen.

"Do you know who the people were who hurt you, boy?" Uncle George asked.

The boy gave his head a slow, negative shake. "A man—a woman," he said.

"But you didn't know who they were?"

The boy opened his mouth as though the words came hard. "I—I never saw the woman before," he said.

"And the man?"

"I—I made a mistake about him," the boy said.

"Mistake?"

"At first—at first I thought it was Mr. Willis from the Academy. But after I heard them talk, I knew it couldn't be. Not Mr. Willis, but someone who looked a little like him."

"You're not sure? Tell me from the beginning."

The boy stirred, moving his legs for the first time.

"After—after they found out what killed Alex I was sure it must have been an accident or—or a crime of some sort. You had gone to New York to see Alex's boss there so—so I couldn't talk to you about it. I knew Alex often cut across the field to get to the Academy after—after we had met on Saturday mornings. I—I decided to go that way to see if there was anything he stopped for, or anyone he saw."

"Good move," Uncle George said.

"But there was nothing," the boy said, his voice breaking as though he was close to tears. "When I got to the boathouse I—I went in. I'd never been in it before. It had been against the rules. So I was in trouble if anyone saw me." The boy's hand shook in Uncle George's hold on it.

"Easy does it, Joey."

"So—so I went in. There was no sign that Alex had been there."

"Why would he gave gone there?" Uncle George asked.

"If he was delivering drugs, like you all said, he could have left what he was carrying there for someone."

"What he was carrying broke open inside his stomach and killed him. You saw that happen, boy," Uncle George said.

"I know, but—but other times, other trips. I wanted to clear him if I could. I—I wanted to be sure."

"So?"

"So—then I heard voices. People coming toward the boathouse from the outside. I—I mustn't be caught there. I squeezed into a kind of locker space, out of sight, but I could see through a sort of grillwork who came in. A woman, and, I thought, Mr. Willis."

"But you weren't sure it was Mr. Willis?"

"I was sure then," Joey said. "But after they talked I knew I must be wrong. It was someone who looked like Mr. Willis—but not Mr. Willis."

"What did they talk about?"

"Some sort of big drug deal," the boy said. "Alex's death might lead the cops onto the trail of it. They were afraid of you." The boy's little smile was crooked. "A smart operator, they called you, Uncle."

"Did they name any names?"

"Yes. Alex—but of course I didn't believe that. Alex's boss in New York, the man you had gone to see, Mr. Ash—some lawyer with a Russian name."

Uncle George's eyes narrowed. "Vulosovich?"

"It—it sounded something like that. All partners they were saying. The time had come to split up some kind of a big money account they had. They made it sound like a million dollars, but of course I didn't believe that. Then it happened."

"What, Joey?"

"When I heard them coming I'd ducked into a locker there. They couldn't see me, I guess because they weren't looking for me, but I could see them through the grillwork in the locker door."

"You said 'it happened'?"

"I—I was sitting on a stool in that locker. It suddenly tipped over and I went down with a crash. The man yanked open the locker door and dragged me out."

"Mr. Willis?"

"The man who looked like Mr. Willis. Mr. Willis couldn't be dealing in drugs, could he?"

"But now you saw him up close."

"I'd never seen Mr. Willis that close," Joey said. "I'd seen him in the village, at sporting events on the Academy playing field. But not close, like eating a meal with someone."

"So then?"

"They knew who I was," Joey said. "Crowder's nephew. They knew I must have heard their whole conversation. I could do them in the woman said. They talked about how to handle me. It—it was scary, because mostly they said I mustn't be allowed to get to you. There was only one way to stop me. The man made a cutting gesture across his throat with his hand." Joey shuddered.

"Oh, my God," Esther said in the background.

"Then they decided I should talk to you on the phone, warn you that if you didn't back away from the case you wouldn't see me again. But you didn't do that. I—I knew you wouldn't back off," Joey said. "I thought if I could tell you where I was, you might be able to save me. I thought I was telling you where I was with 'Friday on Saturday.' The Cogswells'."

"But the boathouse isn't the Cogswells', boy. They sold it to the Academy some time ago," Uncle George said.

"I—I didn't know that."

"I don't imagine you read the real estate ads in the newspaper. So what happened then?" Uncle George asked.

"The man snatched the phone away from me, and I saw him wipe my fingerprints off the receiver."

"Then?"

"He and the woman went over to the far corner of the room. They were going to make sure I didn't hear what they were talking about this time."

"So?"

"I thought there was just a chance I could slip away from them. Outside I could escape from them. I knew the countryside. They didn't, I thought. I—I just ran for the door at the opposite end of the place where they were. The woman saw me and shouted at me to stop. I saw her pick up a knife from the bench in front of her—probably something that was used for trimming sails. I—I just ran."

"If you had stopped, they might have—"

"I didn't stop. I ran. I wanted to get to where I could cross the field to your house. The man had circled around and was coming at me from the other way."

"No way out."

The boy shook his head. "He was armed with some kind of stick. I turned back and the woman was almost on top of me. The man began to hit me over the head with his stick. I—I went down and the lights went out."

"Do you remember the woman jumping on you and stabbing you?"

Joey shook his head. "The last I heard was her shouting at me to stop, but if she got to me I didn't know it. The man had knocked me out with his stick. I didn't know about the stabbing until I woke up in the hospital—heard the doctor talking, and felt the bandages on my chest."

"But you didn't tell them anything?" Uncle George asked.

"I couldn't. I tried when you came, but I couldn't bring it all back into my head. Then after Slick Evarts came and began to tease me with song lyrics, things seemed to start to work again. But so very slowly. I'd have told you what I know now, if I could have."

"You know that your evidence can send them all to prison, probably for life," Uncle George said. "If you can remember it clearly and identify them."

"Prison is not going to be in my future," a voice Uncle George would never forget, came from behind him.

Joshua Willis stood just inside the front door, a handgun pointed directly at Joey. "You don't ever give this boy much of a chance, do you, Crowder? You keep involving him and he is sucker enough to follow your lead. So, he's going to have to go. And your sister and you."

"You think you can get away with it?" Uncle George said.

"I think I can get away with anything in this town," Willis said. "If the boy can't tell his story, I don't have anything to deny, do I? No one else is going to accuse me."

Esther let out a little cry of terror and lunged at the bed, covering Joey's body with her own.

"That just changes the order of things, Mrs. Trimble," Willis said. He smiled at Uncle George. "I see you feeling for that gun I lent you. Don't count on it. It is loaded with blanks for a school play."

Uncle George pulled the gun out of his pocket and fired directly at Willis. Nothing happened. Blanks.

"The ballgame is over, Crowder," Willis said. He aimed his gun at Esther, who was shielding the boy.

"Wait!" Uncle George shouted.

"What for?" Willis asked.

"Some kind of a deal. Our silence," Uncle George said.

"Could I trust you for five minutes?" Willis asked. "Never." He raised his gun and started to bring it down slowly to aim at Esther.

Uncle George knew he couldn't reach him before he pulled the trigger. He had never felt so helpless in his whole life.

From just behind him there came two sharp gunshots. He looked at Esther, a wave of nausea sweeping over him. Leona must have gotten back into the act too soon.

He turned. And there was Red Egan, slowly lowering a smoking gun. Joshua Willis had thrown up his arms, dropped his gun, and fallen to the floor, blood spurting from the side of his head and his face. Uncle George thought he had never seen anyone so dead.

Red Egan, his face grim, slipped his gun into his holster. "Thanks for leaving the kitchen door unlocked, George," he said. "If you hadn't, I'd never have made it."

"What made you think—?"

"I knew you would be here. I came here to tell you we had located the Boyd woman. She had come back to the Academy to get help from Willis, I guess. The cops were still searching for shoes out there and she blundered into them."

154

PATTERN FOR TERROR

Uncle George bent down and put his arm around Esther's shoulder. "It's all right, Es," he said gently. "We are all safe now. Willis is gone, Leona Boyd is under arrest, Ash and Vulosovich, that lawyer, will have to answer to the courts for their part in this."

"Just four people?" Esther asked.

"We'll have to sweep this town from top to bottom for the foot soldiers who were helping," Uncle George said.

Joey propped himself up. "Uncle George, you said Mr. Willis had gone. Where did he go?"

Uncle George's smile was sardonic. "To hell, I expect," he said.